GONE TO SEE
THE RIVER MAN

Kristopher Triana

GRINDHOUSE PRESS

Gone to See the River Man © 2020 by Kristopher Triana. All rights reserved.

Grindhouse Press
PO BOX 521
Dayton, Ohio 45401

Grindhouse Press logo and all related artwork copyright © 2020 by Brandon Duncan. All rights reserved.

Cover design by Lynne Hansen © 2020. All rights reserved.

First published by Cemetery Dance 2020.

Grindhouse Press #071
ISBN-13: 978-1-941918-72-2

This is a work of fiction. All characters and events portrayed in this book are fictitious and any resemblance to real people or events is purely coincidental.

No part of this book may be reproduced, stored in a retrieval system, or transmitted in any form or by any means, including mechanical, electric, photocopying, recording, or otherwise, without the prior written permission of the publisher or author.

Praise for _Gone to See The River Man_ and Kristopher Triana

"Having already proved himself a master of extreme horror with _Full Brutal,_ in _Gone To See The River Man_, Triana shows he is able to paint his uniquely disturbing visions with a much broader palette. This gloomily atmospheric novel is an excellent and unnerving exercise in steadily mounting dread and an inexorable rendezvous with doom. It fuses family tragedy with phantasmagoric horror in a way that will linger long in memory. In short, this Triana guy is a serious contender."

—Bryan Smith, author of _Depraved_

"Such an impressive piece of writing it will rank amongst the best of 2020. You're unlikely to come across a better example of how to build dread over a relatively short page-count."

—_Horror DNA_

"An insanely compelling, addictive storyline that marches right up to the conclusion and bares down on any hope of redemption the reader has left. I was left feeling gutted and at the same time, a sense of urgency to buy more of Kristopher Triana's books."

—_Ginger Nuts of Horror_

"The pacing and character development are stunning not only in skill level, but in how they are used as the vessels for truly transgressive horror moments."

—_Sci-Fi and Scary_

"One of the most exciting and disturbing voices in extreme horror in quite some time. His stuff hurts so good."

—Brian Keene, author of
Earthworm Gods

"_Full Brutal_ is the most evil thing I have ever read. Each book I read by this guy only further convinces me that he's one of the names to watch, an extreme horror superstar in the making."

— Christine Morgan, author of
Lakehouse Infernal

Also by Kristopher Triana

Full Brutal
Blood Relations
The Long Shadows of October
Body Art
The Ruin Season
Shepherd of the Black Sheep
Toxic Love
Growing Dark
The Detained

In loving memory of my mother.

Going to see the river man
Going to tell him all I can
About the ban
On feeling free.

If he tells me all he knows
About the way his river flows
I don't suppose
It's meant for me.

Oh, how they come and go.

—*Nick Drake*

Along a river of flesh
Can these dry bones live?
Take a king or a beggar
And the answer they'll give
Is we're all gonna be, yeah, yeah
I said we're all going to be just dirt in the ground.

— *Tom Waits*

ONE

THERE'S ONLY TWO PLACES ANYONE can find peace—the woods and the grave.

Edmund was almost poetic when he wanted to be, despite his poor grammar and spelling. Lori was actually surprised he'd gotten this sentence out so well. His musings always held some grim underlining, like a black coat of paint beneath a myriad of colors. Or maybe his words just seemed dark because of whose lips they fell from, what he'd done. Lori didn't mind those crimes so much. After all, had it not been for the murders, they never would have started talking to each other.

She read the letter over again. Edmund's handwriting was jagged with large loops, and he dotted everything with an X. The letters were coming more frequently now and were longer in length, this one being four pages. She thought they were building to something unique, something special. She wondered if that crazy Niko woman was getting this many.

Maybe he's writing Niko the exact same ones.

No. Lori couldn't believe that. She refused to. Niko was one of those bizarre people who become romantically infatuated with a killer who has been sensationalized by the media. Things between Lori and Edmund Cox were too deep and complex to be duplicated

GONE TO SEE THE RIVER MAN

with some loon motivated by sexual notoriety and nothing more. Edmund couldn't possibly converse with someone like that the way he had with Lori, even if Niko was a Japanese-American and Lori wasn't. Everybody knew Edmund's preference. Thirteen out of his twenty-one victims had been girls of Asian descent—three Korean, three Chinese, one Vietnamese and six Japanese. The other eight victims could almost pass for Asian, with their dark hair and olive complexions. Lori shared these traits. She was still Edmund's type. But what she shared with him was different. She understood him in ways Niko never could. Of that Lori was certain.

Slipping the letter back into the envelope, she put it in the shoebox with the others. Once this box had held a pair of boots her parents bought her for Christmas. *If they knew the box held my correspondence with Danton's most notorious serial killer now, what would Mom and Dad have to say?*

It was one box of many. The others contained notes, letters, pictures and emails from various serial killers, mass shooters and other convicted murderers she'd started a correspondence with over the years. Her interest in true crime books and documentaries was a hobby turned obsession. It was her one escape from the dullness of her own reality, the emptiness of everyday life that suffocated women far stronger than she was. And personal closeness to such human atrocities brought excitement like a pulsing, electrical charge, a feeling she'd grown addicted to. In conversations with those who took life, Lori no longer felt dead inside. Killers, of all people, made her feel alive.

Lori slipped the "Edmund" box into the bottom drawer of the dresser and tucked it under a pile of neatly folded sweaters. She had an irrational fear of a burglar stealing the letters, selling them to a publisher or collector of serial killer memorabilia. Worse than that, she feared someone might discover, through reading Edmund's letters, just how personal her own letters to him were. They had to be. She had to give these men her stories in exchange for their own because without that intimacy they lost interest. She considered getting a small safe, but money was too tight. She released a long breath. Two in the afternoon and she was still in her house clothes—black stretch pants and a baggy Guns N' Roses T-shirt. Strands of hair had broken free from her ponytail, lining the sides of her face. She glanced at her reflection in the stained window and thought she looked wan, even gaunt.

You'll be forty in six months.

She shook the reminder from her head and turned away as a voice from the other room freed her from her thoughts.

"Sissy?"

Abby still called her that, just as she had when they were kids. It was one of the many childlike traits her sister was unable to let go of, even though she was two years older than Lori.

Lori stepped out into the hall. "Yeah?"

"Is it lunchtime yet?"

Lori rubbed the bridge of her nose. She'd been so lost in her thoughts about Edmund she'd forgotten all about eating. Food wasn't very important to her, but it was to Abby.

"I like sandwiches," Abby said, as if Lori didn't know.

"You want grilled cheese or PB and J?"

Abby was still contemplating when Lori reached the kitchen. Her sister always thought too long and hard over the simplest things. Abby twirled her hair in her fingers and chewed at her bottom lip, brow furrowing beneath her bangs. Lori opened the refrigerator too forcefully. It was hard not to get frustrated with Abby sometimes.

"I'm making PB and J," Lori told her.

"Okay, Sissy."

Abby shuffled to the kitchen counter, her crooked legs struggling as always, her socked feet whispering on the tile like drizzle. She reached to the cabinet and got down her favorite plate, the one with the butterflies on it. She ran her fingertips along the edge, eyes nearly crossing as she smiled at the butterflies as if they were about to spring to life and fly free from the porcelain. Lori made them each a sandwich, opened the baggie of baby carrots and poured two glasses of milk.

"You gonna see your boyfriend today?" Abby asked.

"No. Tomorrow."

"You like him a lot, I guess."

Lori snickered. Unlike Niko, she felt no desire for the man, only intense curiosity. But there was no way of explaining that to her sister.

"You gonna marry him?" Abby asked.

Lori smirked, unsure if Abby was teasing. "I don't know. You think I should?"

Abby stopped chewing. Her face soured in deep thought. Lori waited. She could swear her sister's pupils dilated when she really had to think. It had always been like this, or at least it seemed that way. Lori wiped a dab of jelly from Abby's chin, just above a scar, one of many.

"If people are in love," Abby said, "they've got to get married."

Lori looked down into her milk, idly sliding the glass back and forth. Now she was the one who had to think about what she would say next. What she would tell Abby. What she would tell her co-workers and friends. What she would tell herself.

•••

Lori always arrived twenty minutes early to fill out the paperwork and go through the numerous security clearances. She didn't want any of that nonsense to impede upon the limited time she had to talk with Edmund. It was a miracle enough she was able to get visitations with him. The laws had changed, state by state, and there was talk of in-person visitations becoming a thing of the past in favor of what was referred to as "safer visits" via Skype and other online video platforms. Over the past three months since she'd first visited him in Varden Prison, Lori had gotten the routine down. No revealing clothes; not even shorts. No hats or unconventional garments. No medication, cigarettes or *anything* that could be used as a weapon. Lori brought little with her. That way she could get through the screening easily. She only took in her ID and some money for the vending machine so she could get Edmund his Cheese Doodles and Yoo-hoo. Keeping him happy was one of many actions that helped her one-up her competition when it came to seeing and corresponding with him.

He was already at the table when she entered the room. The sleeves of his shirt were rolled up, revealing hairy forearms and faded, amateur tattoos—skulls, roses, daggers, a battleship. His large hands had done so many things most people would never experience. It made her shiver with a strange combination of fear and awed delight.

His gaze fell upon Lori, sending a second shiver through her. Though not what most would call a handsome man, there was an intensity to Edmund Cox that made him very masculine, a pull that came from beneath the pockmarked cheeks and tombstone gray of his eyes. He smiled at Lori, a possum's grin of yellowed bone. His hair was a tumbleweed and he'd grown two days' worth of stubble. He was every bit as backwoods as where he'd come from.

"Hello darlin'," he said.

Lori tried not to blush as she came toward the table. "Hey, Edmund."

"Brought me some snackies?" he said. She placed them on the table and uncapped the Yoo-hoo for him. "You're always real sweet, aintcha?"

"I like to take care of you."

She knew it was presumptuous but couldn't resist the chance to flirt. She didn't want to lead their relationship in a sexual direction, and yet she had no illusions about him being a male convict and her being a free woman. If she could use her femininity to coax out the darkest inner truths of a killer's conscious, she was not above doing so. It had certainly helped her in her letters. It was a large part of what had gotten her here, sitting before him.

Edmund's hefty body shook as he chuckled. "You are sweet at that. Yes, indeedy."

He took a sip of the Yoo-hoo and when he tilted back his head Lori could see the bullet wound at the base of his neck where a pursuing officer had shot him, putting an end to his killing spree. It made him all the more interesting. His pull was unlike anything she'd ever felt before, an energy that would draw her toward him even when she wanted to resist. It was not charisma or personality; it was energy, raw and visceral and unrelenting, an unstoppable force of nature.

"Ya read my new letter?" he asked.

"Of course." Lori straightened up. The letter had been more serious than the ones before it. It offered her a special opportunity, a way to one-up Edmund's other interested parties. "I read it three times, at least."

He waited for more. "And?"

Lori gripped her knees from the tension, feeling like she was at a job interview, which, in a way, she was. She had never considered herself a writer, but the sort of information Edmund had been exhuming to her about his past could make for a great book deal. Maybe she'd end up being in a documentary like all the ones she binge-watched, a part of true crime history.

"You know I'd do anything for you," she said.

A glint went into the large man's eyes, catching a light that did not exist.

"And so you shall," he said. "You're willing, Lori. That makes you real special. From the first time ya done wrote me, I knew ya were different from them other groupies."

Lori resisted the impulse to wince. She hated that term. *Groupie*. It diminished what she felt she was, or at least aspired to be. She wasn't like Niko. Lori wanted the story, not the man; the truth, not the illusion. Edmund went on, his voice falling deeper.

"That's why I allowed ya—and just a few others—to visit me. You ain't have no idea the amount of mail I get. Much of it's hate mail, but there's a good deal of fans too. I never woulda expected that, but the fan letters came pourin' in pretty much right after I was put in this here cage. I tried to write back to them all, but my writin' ain't so good, and there was just too many. But your letter really stood out."

Lori smiled. She'd spent days working on the letter, drafting and redrafting it on the computer, using what she'd learned from all of her previous correspondences with incarcerated men to craft what she hoped would be the best opening pitch. When she was finally satisfied with it, she printed it out and wrote it all in longhand with a Sharpie pen on crisp, firm paper. It made it feel more personal—a letter from the heart. It reminded her of when she was a teenager in the years before texting and the internet, when passing handwritten notes was commonplace and friends wrote long letters when they were away. She missed that. She missed a lot of things.

"So," Edmund said. "You're acceptin' this ... *quest*, I guess you'd call it."

She took a deep breath. This was it.

"Yes, Edmund. I am honored you trust me to accept it."

His bulk leaned further inward. She could almost smell him now. He was a mélange of body odor—armpits and earwax, blood and dead animal flesh. She noticed his fingernails were packed with dirt.

"You'll find the key in the chest," he said, reiterating the letter's instructions. "You'll find it deep in the low valley of Killen, along the Hollow River, in the shack I done told ya about. The one *they* never knew about."

"You can count on me. I'll bring the key as soon as—"

"Nah. Ya ain't gonna bring it to me. I ain't the one that key belongs to no more, see? Ya gotta take it to The River Man."

That last part had not been in the note.

"Who's that?"

"He lives down river, on the opposite end of the shore from my shack."

Lori shrugged. "But . . . how will I find him? I mean, what's his name? Do you have an address?"

Edmund curled a smile. "He's only The River Man. He ain't on no map. Has a home, but no address. The river is his home. Follow the current down river. You'll find him, just as I did; just as he's gonna find my Lori."

"He's expecting me?"

Edmund nodded. "And you'll know him when ya see him. It's important to always finish what ya started."

Lori's mouth was dry. "Just to clarify, in the letter . . . you said there would be nothing that—"

He held up a hand to stop her. "I ain't askin' ya to continue my murders for me. Ain't askin' ya to hurt anyone or transport no drugs or nothin'. You're returnin' a key . . . or passin' it on. Depends."

"On what?"

"On you."

Lori swallowed. Her throat was like sandpaper, as if she were speaking in front of a large audience. The task had sounded simple at first: get a key from a chest in Edmund's family's old shack in some place called Killen. That had been the extent of the errand, according to the letter. She wanted to do it to see the shack alone, not to mention the benefit of Edmund coming to believe she truly was his friend, someone he could tell anything to. But now she was delivering this key to a hermit who lived down the river, in some barren woodland. On top of that, Edmund was being enigmatic about the whole thing. There was a pinch of hesitation rising through her she had to fight to suppress. She couldn't let her reservations spoil her big chance to make Edmund trust her completely. He wasn't asking Niko to do this, or any of his other, lesser admirers. He'd chosen Lori. She wasn't about to look that gift horse in the mouth, no matter how sharp the teeth may appear.

"All right," she said. "Anything you want."

TWO

SHE COULDN'T LEAVE ABBY ALONE. Lori's sister was incapable of taking care of herself, even for a day or two, which is all Lori guessed the trip to Killen would take. Abby was okay in their apartment when Lori had to go to work, but even then she hated when Lori left and asked repeatedly when she was coming home. It'd taken several talks to keep her from calling the diner every night where Lori waitressed. When Lori started driving for Uber on her days off, she had to have several more talks with her sister about why she couldn't come along on those rides.

This was going to be a much harder discussion.

"You can't come with me, Abby."

Her sister's face pruned. "Sissy! I wanna go too! I don't wanna stay here!"

"You won't be alone, you'll have—"

"No babysitters! I'm not a baby!"

Lori sighed. This trip was for her. Not a vacation by any means, but still a retreat she wanted and needed, a gift she was giving to herself after all the hard work and sacrifices she made on a daily basis just to keep she and Abby from utter ruin. Having her sister there would taint it somehow, or at the very least slow her down.

"It's no fair," Abby said, tears filling her eyes. "You always get to go do fun stuff. I always gotta stay here."

"Fun stuff? You mean like go to work? Serving food and driving people to the airport isn't fun, Abby. This trip isn't going to be big fun either. It's just a walk through the woods. It'll be too difficult for you."

"I wanna go!" Abby sniffled. "I wanna be with Sissy."

Lori sighed harder. When Abby got this way, she stayed in the foul mood until she got what she wanted. She was too mentally limited to comprehend compromise or reason. She would make any caregiver's work impossible. She would go without food and sleep. It would be just one long bout of hysteria until Lori returned. She didn't want to put someone through that, and didn't want to put Abby through it either. She was Lori's responsibility. It was her burden, her curse. She couldn't pass it on to another, not even for a little while.

From looking it up, Lori had learned Killen was a rural river town with a population under five hundred. Edmund told her there were trails to the shack and river, so the hike wouldn't be too treacherous. They could bring Abby's forearm crutches just in case.

Still, she hesitated.

"Abby, what about this—if you be good while I'm gone, I'll take you someplace way more fun next time I have a day off."

Abby's face pinched tighter. She shook her head, hair whipping her cheeks. "Sissy's never off! Never! I'm left alone . . ."

Her words became incoherent sobs as she put her hands to her head. Lori pulled them away before she could dig her nails in, as Abby often did when she had a fit like this, drawing blood without even realizing it.

"Abby! Please—"

"Don't leave, Sissy! Don't leave me like Mommy and Daddy! Don't leave like Petey did!"

•••

Lori had her large hiking backpack and Abby had her purple Sailor

GONE TO SEE THE RIVER MAN

Moon bag. Everything lay on her bed. Abby's medication. Toiletries. Pen and paper. Underwear and socks. Bottled water, snacks and sandwiches. Compass. Pocketknife. Two flashlights and extra batteries. Bear mace—just in case. And most importantly, Edmund's letter of instruction. Abby also insisted on taking her fanny pack, which she liked to fill with small things that made her happy. Abby's lucky rabbit's foot would be coming along, as would her small doggy doll, Mongo. It seemed like almost too much stuff, but Lori would rather have and not need than need and not have. She wasn't sure how long they'd be away.

"An adventure," Abby said with a smile. "Just like in the fort."

Lori nodded. When they were young, they had built a fort out of old pallets their father took from the back of a grocery store. The fort was a rickety, mildewed box of splinters and rusty nails, but to them it had been so many things—a Disney castle, a war bunker, a dining hall for tea parties, a parallel world. It was one of the only times in Lori's life she remembered fondly.

But that was so long ago now; back when things were simple, back when Abby was the big sister in more ways than just her age, back when their little brother was still alive. As always, Lori tried to push Pete so far back in her mind that he would cease to exist, at least for a little while.

"Just like in the fort," Lori said. "And we're gonna find a fort of sorts too. It belongs to my special friend."

Abby snorted. "You mean your boyfriend. You're gonna marry him, right, Sissy?"

Abby smiled. The dentures that filled in for her upper front teeth needed cleaning. Lori would have to take care of that before they left. There was always a twinkle in Abby's eyes when Lori talked about Edmund. It offered a glimpse of the girl Lori had grown up with, just enough to make her wish for lucidity to return to her sister again, though she knew it was a wish without hope. If there had been that lucidity, Abby would already know who Edmund Cox was. She would have seen it on the news or read it in the paper. But Abby wasn't interested in watching the news. She preferred cartoons and musicals. And she never read anymore, though she loved when Lori read to her. She didn't know what Edmund had done, didn't understand what he was.

"Maybe I'll marry him," Lori teased. "Maybe."

"You're gonna. I know you are. You're in love."

"Well, if I do marry him, I want you to be my maid of honor."

Abby blinked, her eyelids out of sync. "What's that?"

"It's the bride's most important friend."

Abby grinned, the scar on her chin stretching like taffy, growing nearly as big as the one on her forehead where her skull had split open.

"I'm Sissy's best friend," she said.

Lori wrapped one arm around her sister and when Abby tucked into her like a beloved pet, she kissed the top of her head. She was more than a best friend. She was Lori's only family.

•••

The rain added an additional layer of gray to an already dismal October morning. It brought a deeper chill with it, the dampness driving the cold into their bones. The sisters drove with the heat on low, but Abby needed her window cracked so she wouldn't get carsick. Wisps of air jetted through, cutting Lori's skin like icicles. Already she wanted inside the cabin. She imagined it as a cozy, little house of logs, a place Edmund might spend winter nights snuggling in if things were different. Dawn had come and gone, but the weather made it seem like it was lingering in an impasse, that daylight would never come. Sweet birch and sugar maples lined the state road, their wet branches hanging overhead, creating a spotty, russet tunnel of foliage, the branches clawing the sky. They had just entered Killen but hadn't seen another car for almost forty-five minutes.

"It's like a fairy story," Abby said.

"What is?"

GONE TO SEE THE RIVER MAN

"The woods here. I think they must be magical, don't you, Sissy?"

Abby twirled her rabbit's foot between her fingers, patting the same spot where she'd long ago worn out the fur. She was wearing her pink Boston Red Sox baseball cap with her hair in a ponytail sticking out the back. Abby didn't watch baseball. She just loved the color and the letter B. *It's a letter and the name of a bee too, Sissy.*

"I guess we'll have to find out," Lori said. "Magic is always where you least expect it."

She liked that Abby was excited by the woods instead of intimidated. Things would be a lot easier if her sister wasn't afraid. She didn't respond to fear well. Lori had seen it overtake her so many times before. The medication made these bouts of inexplicable terror less frequent, but no less extreme when they fell upon Abby like a swarm of army ants. Over the years, Lori had figured out ways to calm her sister down, but sometimes getting Abby back to earth was slow going, and it always broke Lori's heart all over again.

The road wound like a serpent through the low hills, the Ford's tires making soft white noise of the rainy streets, whispers bouncing off of concrete. Lori turned on the radio but found mostly static. The only station that came through was dedicated solely to the blues. She kept it low—Howlin' Wolf singing about living in the woods, Skip James whispering about a hard time killing floor. It wasn't until a song called "You Better Run" came on that she switched the radio off. The lyrics to Junior Kimbrough's hypnotic tune unsettled Lori, especially around her sister, the song being about an attempted rape at knifepoint. The sound of the autumn air rushing through the windows was a welcomed change. Mist rose up from the valley in a white squall, assuring the river was not far away, fog drifting through the mountains like a dreary dream.

Edmund's words returned to her.

I ain't the one the key belongs to anymore. You gotta take it to The River Man.

Lori straightened up, hands a little tighter on the wheel. She nibbled at a cuticle and told herself her skin was only prickling because of the breeze coming through the window. All last night she had tossed in bed, deciding not to go through with Edmund's strange request, then changing her mind. She drifted in and out of a light sleep broken by stress nightmares of getting lost in the woods and losing sight of Abby. Lori figured it was only natural to be anxious, even a little worried. Who knew who this River Man was? He didn't even have a proper name, at least not one Edmund cared to mention. If this mystery man was a friend of his, did that mean he was into the same things Edmund had been into—the violence, the rape and the butchering? Now that they were more than just pen pals, she liked to believe Edmund cared about her, or at least didn't want to lose her. His letters were very forward and suggestive. He made it clear he wanted more than a platonic relationship, especially if Lori led him on. It didn't make sense for him to put her in harm's way. But that didn't guarantee this recluse in the woods wouldn't hurt her, did it? And what about Abby? Maybe she should have left her at home after all.

But it was too late for that now. If she didn't get the key in a timely fashion, Edmund might grow impatient and turn over the quest to Niko. The key brought up more questions now that she wasn't bringing it to Edmund. What did the key unlock? Why did Edmund have it if it belonged to someone else? She hadn't dared ask. It would have come off as untrusting, and that would be counterproductive to the whole damn point of this.

Winding around a sharp corner, the trees opened like a starving mouth, revealing their first glimpse of the Hollow River. The waters ran slow but steady, a greenish-gray current lurking behind dense fog that sluiced through the surrounding thicket like dry ice vapor, dilating with each falling raindrop.

"Are we going sailing, Sissy?"

"No, Abby. Just hiking along the riverside."

GONE TO SEE THE RIVER MAN

"We're gonna go to your boyfriend's fort. We can play castle there, just like we used to, 'member? I know we're grown up now, but I was just thinking, you know? We can have a tea party with Mongo. Just for, what you call, like, old times." She looked to the backseat where the plush dog poked out of the top of her backpack where he was zippered in. "I dunno if real dogs like tea, but I think we should have a tea party if we're gonna be in a fort, don't you, Sissy? Just like when we were little."

Lori reached over and patted her sister's hand. It was cold, bony. Though slow, Abby didn't have any illusions about the fact that she was a forty-two-year-old woman. She liked childish things but wasn't prone to childish games or fantasy. But she was sentimental about the lives they'd had thirty years ago, and while Lori wasn't, she supposed she could see why. Abby seemed to understand, in a way, that she had been different back then, and Lori suspected that deep down her sister longed to be that way again.

"We'll see how the shack is," Lori said. "If it's clean enough, we can have a little picnic there and eat our lunches. How's that?"

Abby smiled, but there was something sad behind her eyes, a dimming of disappointment. Lori almost told her they could play while they were there but stopped just before it could come out. She didn't want to waste any time while they were in these woods. They'd brought sleeping bags in case they would need them, but she was hoping to get the key to The River Man before dark. If they were going to be out of the woods by sunset, there would be no time for dillydallying.

•••

The rain seemed to be enjoying itself. It hammered down and then turned to drizzle, then back again, showing off as they went around the last curve before the pavement ended. The muddiness of the dirt road made Lori apprehensive to drive much farther. The car was two-wheel drive and needed new tires, as well as brakes and rotors and a whole mess of other things she couldn't afford. They would get stuck if they pressed on much farther, and the river was in sight, maybe a quarter mile from where they were. She pulled to the side of the road and parked under a canopy of maples that bent from the weight of the storm.

"It's raining, Sissy."

"I know. We have our raincoats. We'll be okay."

Lori reached over to the backseat where they lay, hers a practical gray one that went down to the waist, Abby's a yellow Dick Tracy-like slicker that made her look like a fisherman. They'd worn boots. Hopefully Abby would be able to trench through the mud okay.

"Alright," Lori said, "let's get these coats on and get the gear outta the trunk."

Lori watched her sister as she stepped through the muck, but Abby seemed to be walking without any more than her usual struggle to do so. They retrieved their packs and Lori attached the sleeping bags to the poles of her larger, sturdier pack, the one she'd used while camping with Matt before he'd tired of her like all the others. He was an outdoorsman and taught her a good deal about being in the wilderness, little tips and techniques that may go to good use now.

She missed Matt sometimes. He'd been her last real boyfriend and left her over five years ago. Now the effort it took to find someone new just wasn't worth it. She'd replaced physical intimacy with men for a sort of mental intimacy, the kind she'd been developing with Edmund.

"It's rainy, Sissy."

"I know. You already said that."

Sometimes her sister's redundancy grated on Lori's nerves. She couldn't let it get to her today. There were enough challenges ahead without petty aggravations.

Closing up the car, Lori put up the hood of her raincoat and pulled the shoulder straps of her backpack higher, gripping them in her hands. She turned to the long road of sludge and pebbles that wound down into the valley below like a stream of brown blood—the blood of the woods, the blood of the world. Dying trees lined the path, branches swaying in gentle wind, waving to Lori and Abby, welcoming them into their embrace.

"Come on."

Lori walked but didn't hear any footsteps behind her. She turned to see Abby standing in place. She was facing the river, staring at it. Not even off the road yet and already she seemed lost.

"Abby, come on. We have to get to the trail."

Her sister looked back at her but said nothing.

"Dontcha wanna get to the fort?"

Abby looked at the ground, mulling it over. She nodded.

"Okay. Then let's get moving."

She took Abby's upper arm in her hand, guiding her sister, confused by the hesitation she saw on her face. But then, Abby didn't always make sense. Brain damage took her places no one else could understand. The caverns of her mind could swallow her now and then, sometimes bringing the unprovoked terrors, other times initiating a state of near catatonia. They couldn't afford one of those spells now. It was too soon to give Abby her next dose of medication, but maybe in an hour or so.

"How long's it gonna rain, Sissy?"

Lori exhaled relief. Abby was speaking again. She took it as a good omen.

THREE

DEAREST EDMUND,

Your last letter really moved me, perhaps even more so than the other ones. You have a way of expressing yourself that is very unique, and obviously your story touches me. It makes me angry that your side of the story has never been told to the world. Maybe it would give people a better understanding of why you had to do what you did.

We've all done mean things to other people. I know you said you don't feel bad about your crimes, but I have many regrets for the people I've hurt over the years. I've broken people's hearts, let them down. I hurt them without intending to, but hurt them nonetheless. My motivations don't change their pain any more than your motivations change the pain of those you've hurt. The people we make suffer stay inside of us longer and more deeply than those who we bring joy, don't you think? They are our personal crosses to bear. At least, that's the way I feel. I know you feel differently, but I also know you carry those you hurt with you in another way. You took them, making them yours forever. That's what you've said. I think there's a sort of love in that. Most people would never see it that way, but I do.

GONE TO SEE THE RIVER MAN

That's because I understand you in all the ways they don't. We are kindred spirits, you and I. We have a deeper understanding of pain and our own dark sides. You've faced yours full on. I've yet to be that strong. That's all the more reason I need you in my life. I think you can guide me through whatever it is that clouds my mind and makes me shut down whenever the past comes looking for me.

These other women who come to you only want you for your fame. They want to be somebody through you, to take advantage of your accomplishments. I'm not like them and I think you know that. I can feel it with every letter you write. The connection grows stronger with every word. There's so much deeper we can go together. Maybe as one we can get to the heart of all things. Maybe there's peace there. Maybe's there's something more.

Yours,
Lori

FOUR

THERE WAS MOVEMENT ON THE edge of the forest.

Something black. Something big.

Lori held her breath without realizing she was doing so and reached back for Abby, guiding her off the roadway and into a small grove of trees.

Abby twitched. "Sissy?"

"*Shh.* Don't say anything."

The rain had let up to a mist. Lori watched the shape as it wandered through the lingering fog and slung off her backpack to retrieve the bear mace. The shape kept moving forward, coming down the road in their direction. The sisters crouched and Abby started whispering something, but Lori shushed her again. She squinted against the mist obscuring the shape. It seemed to be going in and out of focus. It blurred before her eyes as if tears clouded them.

It's too tall to be a bear. Lori started breathing again, still squinting as the figure took shape. Realizing it wasn't an animal, she got to her feet, but Abby stayed crouched in the mud, her legs twisted, awkward. Lori hoped she hadn't paralyzed her sister with fear. She whispered to her that it was okay, but Abby didn't appear to be listening. Her eyes were locked on the man coming down the road.

"Get up," Lori said. "Everything's fine."

GONE TO SEE THE RIVER MAN

Something sharp nagged at the back of Lori's mind, telling her she didn't know if that were true. They were in the middle of nowhere, two women alone, and here was a man walking through a rainstorm by himself. He was tall but skinny, dressed in a black suit and hat. It was a country gentleman's Wilton with a long brim that hid his features. He wore a white, ruffled tuxedo shirt that had gone gray with rain, the cuffs of which hung long out of his coat sleeves and cloaked his hands.

"Never mind," she told her sister. "You stay hidden in there a minute, okay?"

Abby nodded, watching on, unblinking.

Lori started up the dirt road, keeping the bear mace in hand but tucked into the pocket of her raincoat. The rain had soaked through her jeans by now and a deeper chill had sunk into her bones. She glanced at the sky. Despite the downpour turning to mist again, she saw no sign of the storm coming to an end. Bloated clouds were on the verge of going black, churning overhead like a witch's cauldron, a groan of distant thunder rolling deep within them.

When she glanced back at the man, he was looking right at her. Lori gasped. She could see his face now, his terrible grin. His lips peeled back from their gums, teeth appearing bigger than normal due to shriveled flesh that clung corpse-like to his skull. He was withered with age, in his late eighties at the very least. Pale eyes watched her from out of cavernous pits of grayed flesh. He moved slowly and with extra effort, slightly bent at his lower back, arms swinging ape-like as he shuffled along. He lifted one and waved, long fingers emerging from his shirtsleeves as if rising from a grave.

"Mornin', mah dear!" His voice was high and fluttery. "And what a mornin' it is."

Lori nodded a hello. "Good mornin'."

She realized she'd stopped walking, but the man kept moving on, and the closer he came the taller he seemed, the more yellow his teeth, the more scraggly the white hair that hung down to his shoulders.

"Saints alive," he said. "Looks like you're ready for a *long* journey."

Lori tried to give a friendly smile but worried that it came off all wrong, so she gave it up. Neutrality was the best she could come up with. The old man pointed over her head to her backpack, his smile growing impossibly wider.

"Oh," she said. "Right. Yeah, a journey, sort of. I guess."

"Road gives out up a spell. You must be headin' down to the ol' Hollow."

She nodded. The man was only a few feet away from her now. He stopped walking just as she was about to step back.

"The ol' Hollow's a-risin' with this'n here rain," he said. "Sometimes I think she'll grow big 'nough to swallow all of Killen. Lord knows how it swallows."

Lori searched for words that would not come. "Um . . ."

"But maybe that wouldn't be so bad, now would it? This town could use a baptism. What little is left of it anyways." He paused and Lori thought he was about to introduce himself, but he went on. "Ain't too many good folk left 'round these parts nowadays. Reckon it wouldn't be much a shame to lose those who've stayed behind in a place like this. What kinda decent folk would stay in a Sodom like Killen?"

Lori shifted uncomfortably. "Sorry?"

"Ain't nothin' you need to be sorry for. Or is there?" His smile was like a set of shark teeth, huge and ominous. "You tell me."

"I have to get going."

Lori moved into the center of the road.

The man's eyes flashed. "Wouldn't do that."

"Why not?"

"Well, you wouldn't wanna leave your friend behind now, would ya?"

Something went tight in Lori's neck. "What?"

GONE TO SEE THE RIVER MAN

The old man shook his head and let out a wet click of a laugh. "You have two sleepin' bags on your back, child. You ain't travelin' alone. But I guess no one really goes down this river alone, now do they? Even when they go by themselves, they ain't never truly *alone*. You're carryin' more than that pack, that's for sure."

"Look, mister. I don't—"

"Can't go empty-handed. Not when ya gone to see The River Man."

Lori tensed. "You don't know where we're going."

"Only one place this ol' river gonna take a traveler."

Lori crossed her arms. The last thing she wanted was for this creep to know where she and Abby were headed, but he might be her only opportunity to learn more about where she was headed in the first place.

"Who is this River Man anyway?" she asked. "You know him?"

The old man gazed off into the forest. "Ya'll have a nice visit. I know I did."

He commenced his shuffling, and though his eyes fell beneath the dripping rim of his hat as he passed by, his smile remained. The spaces between his teeth seemed thicker now, blacker. Lori looked at the tiny rips and tears that covered his soggy suit. In one of the holes in his shoulder, she thought she saw movement—an insect or worm. He moved into the center of the road, stooped and swaying as he passed by the grove where Abby was hidden. Lori followed, her jaw hard, the bear mace held tighter in her fist. But the old man just kept on walking. He didn't even glance in the direction of the grove, only up at the sky as he sang to the clouds, his singing voice like that of a child.

"*Yes, we'll gather at the river! The beautiful, beautiful river! Gather with the man at the river . . .*"

•••

"Who was he, Sissy?"

"I don't know. Just a guy."

The old man was out of sight and Abby had emerged from her hiding spot. She'd been kneeling and now her jeans were caked in mud.

"Where's he going?"

"I don't know, Abby."

"Is he lost?"

Lori shook her head. "Don't think so."

But maybe her sister was on to something. The man might have dementia. Maybe he had wandered away from a nursing home. He was very old and hadn't been making much sense. Maybe Lori's uneasiness around him had been misplaced. He had creeped her out, but maybe that was more due to the situation than anything he'd done. At his age, how much trouble could he have really caused them? The poor man couldn't even stand up straight.

So what was he doing out here? Had his car broken down? Did he live nearby? He was walking—*shuffling*—down a muddy road in the middle of nowhere. It seemed crazy, but wasn't Lori doing the exact same thing? Did Abby walk with any more ease than the old-timer did?

Lori stopped. The road had ended, or at least had thinned to a trail. They'd reached the path that dropped into the densely wooded bowels of the valley. The land was mountainous and rust-colored, jutting with large rocks and littered by trees fallen long ago. River mist crept across the land like a swarm of spiders. The thunder groaned. Lori looked around until she saw the sign Edmund had told her to watch for, finding it tucked behind the overhanging branches of a dying bush. It was a small wooden plank carved into an arrowhead, nailed into a yard sign's post. Bold letters in red spray paint greeted them.

INTO THE HOLLOW, it read.

FIVE

PETE HELD HIS HAND TO his forehead, shielding his eyes from the blinding August sunshine. It was hot today—almost too hot to play outside—but he was too excited to be included to ever complain. His older sisters rarely wanted to do anything with him anymore. Lori was twelve now, practically a teenager. Abby was fourteen and a half, and she always reminded you of the half. Being only ten, Pete was made to feel like a little baby. Not just by his sisters, but by his parents too. It wasn't until this summer that they allowed him to go off into the woods to play with his sisters without adult supervision. It seemed to Pete that Lori and Abby had always played in the woods while he had to stay in the yard, playing G.I. Joe alone in the fort while they went on all sorts of adventures. Now he was actually allowed to tag along with them. It made him feel not only older, but cooler, like he was part of a club meant for the big kids, one he'd managed to get into only because his sisters vouched for him. He only wished he'd worn shoes instead of going barefoot. The woods were not as yielding as the lawn.

He heard the water before he saw it. At first he thought the sound was passing cars, but they were far from any road. They were deep in the forest now. He'd been following his sisters without looking back. Now that he did, a tremor rippled through him, hinting at the first pinpricks of fear.

"Come on, Pete."

He blinked out of his reverie to see he'd stopped walking. Abby was calling to him from farther ahead. She had grown so much taller in the past year and her gangly body looked almost cartoonish as she held her arms out, balancing from rock to rock. When she smiled her retainer shimmered in the light, and the bottom of her cropped shirt fluttered, revealing the soft, white flesh of her belly. Pete smiled back, watching his sister's ponytail whip as she bobbed her head from side to side.

"Move your butt," Abby said. "We're almost there."

Pete didn't know where "there" was or what awaited them when they arrived; he just knew he was excited to get to it. His sisters told him so many stories about the woods. In his mind, it was a place of limitless possibilities, like something out of a fable. Now that he heard the aquatic sound his heart began to quicken, his fear of being so far from home breaking under the wonder of what lay ahead.

"I'm comin'!" he said, picking up the pace.

Abby hopped off a stone and trotted through the grass to catch up with their sister. Lori had kept on walking, not waiting for anyone. She was like that sometimes. It was one of the reasons Pete liked Abby better. Lori was fine most days but would get into moods where she'd be cold to Pete for no real reason. She also wasn't as fun as Abby was, and nowhere near as popular. Abby had a large circle of friends and always seemed to be at the center of them. Lori, on the other hand, seemed to shy away from crowds. She wasn't an outcast. She had friends of her own but seemed to value them less, and they seemed to return the favor.

Pete's friends meant everything to him. He wanted to be liked. He wanted to be popular. And though he loved Lori, he more than just loved Abby; he wanted to be like her. She was the coolest person he knew, and he was lucky enough to be related to her. And now he was being introduced to other parts of her incredible world.

GONE TO SEE THE RIVER MAN

Pete followed down the trail, swatting at gnats and licking the sweat that had made a dew mustache on his upper lip. Abby climbed over the fallen tree blocking the trail, whereas Pete chose to crawl under it. He was caught up to her now. Giggling, Abby broke into a jog, and Pete couldn't help but notice there was a bounce where her small breasts had budded.

"Come on, already!" Lori called from nowhere.

She was so far ahead of them Pete couldn't see her anymore. Why did she have to go so fast? Why couldn't she wait up? He was tempted to tell Mom and Dad on her, but quickly discarded the idea. That was the sort of thing a little baby would do.

The sound of rushing water grew louder. He smelled something fresh as ice. Passing through the last bit of thicket, he met up with his sisters where they stood at the edge of the cliff overlooking the stream. They'd had heavy rain the past few weeks, the summer storms like clockwork, and the stream was a rowdy, living thing, its waters raging against the black rocks. Lori stood closest to the edge, holding a wooden plank in her hands that hung from a mold-green rope tied to an overhanging branch of the red maple. Pete inched toward the edge and looked down, feeling dizzy. The water seemed so far away, like he was watching it from the window of a ten-story building. He swallowed and looked at Lori.

"Is that a swing?" he asked.

Lori smirked. "Yeah. What else would it be?"

"But it swings out over the creek!"

"No duh."

Lori straddled the plank, the rope between her thighs and clenched in both fists. Pete picked at his fingers without looking at them. He wanted to scream at her not to do it, but at the same time he sort of wanted to see it. It was scary, but also looked fun, like a rickety rollercoaster.

"I'm next," Abby said.

She flung off her T-shirt, revealing the bikini top Pete hadn't known she'd been wearing under her clothes. Lori was still in her shorts and New Kids on the Block T-shirt. Had she worn a bathing suit too? Pete only had on his tighty-whities underneath his cutoff jeans. But he wasn't planning on swimming. How would they even get down there?

Suddenly the thought hit him.

They're going to jump off the swing.

This was even crazier than he'd thought. He assumed they would just swing over the stream, like a daredevil jumping a motorcycle over flaming cars. He hated to be the killjoy. It was asking to be left behind from now on. But his fear got the better of him. Of all the nightmares he frequently suffered, the ones involving falling terrified him the most. He'd toss in his sleep so hard he would often actually fall out of bed. He preferred that because it woke him up. Better that than let the night terrors of falling continue.

"Are you guys nuts?" he asked. "You'll break your legs!"

Abby rolled her eyes. "We've done it, like, a million times, Petey."

"Yeah," Lori said. "It's fun. It's right over the clear spot where there aren't any rocks. You're safe as long as the water's high and it's rained every day."

She reared back, the rope going taut as she prepared for launch. Pete's heart accelerated. He stepped forward.

"Wait!"

He thought for sure Lori would ignore him. She often did. But to his surprise, she stopped and looked at him. She even smiled.

"It's okay, Pete. Seriously."

But he just couldn't believe that. Even if they'd swung out over the stream before, he felt certain they would get seriously injured this time. He went to Lori and took her arm, pulling her off the swing and away from the cliff.

"Pete . . ."

"You're gonna get hurt!"

GONE TO SEE THE RIVER MAN

Abby walked by in a huff. "For God's sake, Pete, don't be a wussy."

Pete felt tight in the chest, not used to harsh words from her. The last thing he wanted to be thought of was a chicken. That was even worse than being branded a baby. Abby mounted the swing, leaving not a second for him to protest, and swung out over the crashing water below. Pete's breath left him as he watched her spin in the sky. Then she let go of the rope. For a moment she seemed to hover in midair before her plummet back to earth. Pete and Lori raced to the edge of the cliff. Abby was falling feet first, screaming without sounding frightened. When she hit the water, Pete gasped. Lori cheered. A moment later Abby's head emerged from the stream. She was laughing.

"See?" she called up. Her voice echoed off the rock walls of the mountain. "It's fun, Pete! Come on! You're next!"

Pete stepped back from the edge. Though Abby was okay, his trepidation persisted. The swing was still swaying back and forth, an ominous pendulum.

"Wanna try it?" Lori asked. "I'll help you do it carefully. You have to aim your jump when the swing is all the way out, that way you avoid the rocks."

He looked at his sister. Her face was warm, understanding in a way she rarely showed. She suddenly reminded him of his mother.

"I dunno . . ."

From below, Abby called out. "Pete! Stop being such a wimp!"

He kept his voice low. "I don't think I can do it."

Lori put a hand on his shoulder. "S'okay. You don't have to."

Relief washed over him. He'd thought the girls were going to gang up and pressure him. He thought of something Dad often said whenever Pete was copying his classmates in order to fit in. *If your friends were jumping off a cliff, would you do that too?*

Abby yelled from below. "Pete! Come on!"

"No!" he shouted. "I'm not doing it!"

"Lori! Put him on the swing and push him over!"

Fear slithered up his spine once again. He looked at Lori, but she was going to the edge by herself. She cupped her hands around her mouth.

"Just leave him alone, Abby!"

"Are you serious?" Abby called up. "He needs to be a man sometime, right?"

"He'll do it when he's ready to. I'm not gonna push him!"

"Fine! I'll come back up and do it myself!"

"No you won't!"

But Abby didn't reply. Listening to the sound of her exiting the water, Pete crossed his arms in a self-hug.

"Don't worry," Lori said.

Having her in his corner gave him a bit more confidence. It was strange to suddenly like Lori better than Abby, at least at this moment. He was grateful for her support and made a note to not forget this the next time she was being a butthead.

Abby made it to the top faster than he expected.

She sneered at him. "You're such a turd."

"Leave him alone," Lori said. "Don't be a bully."

"Hey! I'm not a bully."

"Then stop acting like one. Stop trying to make him do it."

Abby threw up her hands. "Fine. Whatever."

They didn't speak the rest of the way home.

SIX

THERE WERE MISSING PLANKS IN the bridge; only ropes for handrails. But it wasn't high off the ground. Lori figured Abby could manage, but she would go slow anyway and stick close to her. Below them, a shallow creek gurgled, sluicing between the rocks, reminding Lori of things she'd rather not remember. She wondered if Abby remembered them or if her damaged mind had been mercifully wiped clean of such bad memories.

The thunderstorm released a light drizzle. The trail was wide in some spots, nearly overgrown in others, the dying brush of autumn scraping at their heels as they marched on. Most of the hike had been on flat land, with only a few hills to climb, none too steep. But ahead the trail wound into the mountain. She hoped they would find Edmund's shack without a struggle. Abby could only take so much.

"This bridge is shaky, Sissy."

"Just hold on to the ropes and keep your eyes on your feet. Watch for the gaps in the wood."

Abby held the rope rail with one hand but kept the other on Lori's backpack. The trickling water gave off an additional chill. The fragrance of wet, dead leaves made Lori feel lighter, and she daydreamed of going apple-picking the way she and Matt had in the fall. She wondered if Edmund enjoyed things like that and then she shook her head, annoyed by her own mind's musings. What the hell did it matter if Edmund liked picking fruit? That's not what she wanted to learn about him. Besides, he was going to spend the rest of his life in prison. His days of autumnal activities were over.

The bridge began to shake beneath them. Her sister giggled.

"Abby, stop bouncing."

Abby kept giggling but didn't wobble the bridge any further. When they reached the end Lori took Abby's hand and helped her cross back to land.

"Are we there?" Abby asked.

"Not yet. You need a break?"

Abby nodded. Her eyes were downcast and her mouth hung open.

"Okay then."

Lori led her to a fallen eastern hemlock tree that had taken a huge chunk of earth with it. Its exposed roots were a wooden squid reaching in every direction, the mound of dirt beneath it like the mouth of a cave. They slung off their backpacks and sat on the middle of the tree.

"Want a snack?" Lori asked.

"Nah. I wanna wait 'til we get to the fort. Then we can have snackies." Abby opened her fanny pack and retrieved her rabbit's foot. She rubbed it, watching her fingers move across the spotted white fur that had grayed from various stains.

"How come your boyfriend don't come to our apartment?"

Lori turned to her sister, surprised, unsure how to answer. "It's complicated."

Abby's brow furrowed. Complication was not easy for her to wrap her mind around.

"Does he not wanna meet me?" she asked.

"No, no." Lori rubbed circles on Abby's back. "It's not that at all."

GONE TO SEE THE RIVER MAN

Abby looked at her with sad, dark eyes. "Do you not want him to meet me?"

"Abby—"

"You scared he won't like me and then he won't like you?"

"Abby, stop it, come on. You're being ridiculous. Edmund is in a place he can't leave right now. Okay?"

Abby pursed her lips, frog-like. "Like, a hospital?"

Lori shrugged. "Sort of."

"I don't like hospitals."

"I know."

Abby had spent many months in Regional Care, learning to walk again, or at least shuffle brokenly. Lori would never forget the sight of her collapsing the first few times she tried to move on her own. There were pads beneath her in the physical therapy room, but she'd screamed like she was being murdered. She'd had so much fear back then. So had their parents. Fear and anger and grief. Lori had worried they would never be the same family again. Over time, those worries were validated. The family had shattered just as easily as Abby's bones.

"Can I go meet him when we get back?" Abby asked. "I don't like hospitals, but I wanna meet him."

Lori hated the idea. "I'll see what I can do."

"Sissy is gonna marry him one day. And I get to be the maid."

Lori chuckled. "Maid of honor, silly. Maid of honor."

"On who?"

Lori pulled her sister close, hugging her shoulders. "You goofy grape."

Abby laughed, light and high, the sound of a young girl in summer who's running through a lush field, then leaping, floating in the air, soaring through the sky like ash, never to be that young again.

Abby's legs hurt. She tried to move in a way that didn't hurt her knees as much, but that just made her ankles hurt. But she didn't want to make Sissy sad or angry. She was always worried about being an even *badder* sister than she already was. She couldn't say this, or even understand it, but the bad feeling was there, a dark blue pool of doubt she often sank into. Lately she'd been sinking more than ever.

Sissy had a new boyfriend. It made Abby worry. Though she couldn't remember why, something about Sissy having a boy around made Abby's stomach hurt. Even rubbing her lucky rabbit's foot didn't make it go away. Boyfriends meant trouble. Was that why Sissy kept saying he wasn't really a boyfriend? Was she just trying to make Abby feel better? Did she not want Abby to know something? That was the way it felt to her. Secrets. Bad secrets. For Abby and Sissy, boyfriends were bad news! Thinking about them made Abby twitchy-itchy, and she bit at her nails without even knowing it. Sometimes Sissy pushed her hands from her mouth and put something yucky on them so Abby wouldn't do it. But she did it anyway. She couldn't stop.

Before, she was happy about getting to be the maid-off-on-her, but now she didn't want any wedding at all, because if Sissy married the boy, would Abby still be loved? Would Sissy want to throw Abby away so she could run away with him? She wanted to be happy for big Sissy. Being in love made people super happy. But now she was in the woods, and the woods were spooky. They said scary things. About Sissy and the boy. They made Abby cold and she didn't know where home was anymore, if home was anywhere in the world now. It made her super sad. Then it made her mad.

She missed Mommy and Daddy. She missed Petey. She didn't want to miss Sissy that way.

Sissy was supposed to stay with Abby.

Stay forever.

•••

It was almost four o' clock. Lori's stomach was beginning to devour itself. It roared audibly, making Abby giggle and say that her belly monster was singing. They'd been walking for hours and the terrain had grown more resistant with aboveground roots and uphill challenges. They were moving closer along the river now, the trail overlooking it. Green waves lapped at the shoreline like reptile tongues, the clouds groaning overhead. Lori was feeling the strain, so she knew Abby must be suffering, and yet her sister hadn't complained.

"Let's take a lunch break," Lori said.

Abby's face soured with hurt. "But the fort!"

"Abby, I'm starving. You should've had your medicine an hour ago. You know you need to eat with it."

"You promised we could go to the fort, Sissy!"

"We *are* going to the fort. But we need something to eat to hold us over and keep us energized."

Abby pouted. Her breath quickened, growing shallow. "You... said . . ."

"Calm down—"

". . . the fort . . ."

"Abby, you need to breathe."

Lori put her hands on Abby's shoulders but her sister shook free of her. Lori was so startled she fell back, barely catching herself as her feet slid in the mud. Abby was on the verge of hyperventilating. Her face was going pink. Still-damp hair stuck to her forehead and eyebrows, her false teeth flashing like the lightning.

"Abby, listen to me. You need to calm down."

Her sister snarled, an expression Lori hadn't seen on Abby's face in decades. She'd been angry plenty of times since the accident but had never directed that anger right at Lori. Now she was curling her lip with a grudge. Her face went tight, eyes like cold, dead moons.

"Fuck you, Lori."

Now it was Lori who forgot to breathe. She couldn't remember the last time she'd heard Abby use vicious profanity. *Shit* was usually her limit. And she hadn't called her *Sissy*. Instead she'd used her name. It seemed colder somehow.

"What's gotten into you?" Lori asked.

Her sister crossed her arms and turned away.

"Abby? Are you all right? You never talk like this."

"Yeah, well . . ."

She trailed off, staring at the rocky shore below. Lori went to her. This time Abby didn't pull away.

"Look," Lori began, "I'm sorry, okay? I didn't realize it meant so much to you to wait to eat until we got there. The map he made says we're not far. Seems like it's said that forever, but hopefully we'll see the shack when we get over this next hill. We can hold off on lunch if you want. Just bite a protein bar once and take your pills, okay?"

Abby's eyes left the river. "Alright."

Lori took a deep breath as their relationship came back to reality. She still didn't know what to make of Abby's uncharacteristic outburst, but they had to move on if they were ever going to eat. Maybe she could blame the meltdown on her missing medicine time. It was easier than thinking about it right now.

Abby took a tiny nibble from the protein bar, washed down her pills with water and returned focus to the trail, Lori leading the way, hoping they were still headed in the right direction. The trail had not forked, and they hadn't veered off it. Or so she thought. Still, she felt lost. The backpack seemed to weigh thirty pounds more than it had when they'd started, and the straps were irritating her shoulders. She kept repositioning them, but they always fell right back into the sore spots when she moved. She was tempted to munch on trail mix, leaving the sandwiches alone for now, but didn't want to risk another tantrum from her sister. Abby's *fuck you* had pained her, and she knew the shock would linger, a shit stain on her consciousness. She chewed on her lip and pressed on, the air growing meaner, the sky more miserable.

She tried to think of Edmund and his story, of all she stood to gain from this trip, but her mind kept drifting away from intrigue

GONE TO SEE THE RIVER MAN

and into black thoughts of hopelessness. Edmund wasn't the only one who would never pick apples again. If Lori were to go, she would do so alone or with her sister, like some spinster incapable of taking a new lover. She would never pick apples with a man again, never make love under the stars or kiss atop a Ferris wheel. The only man in her life was a maniac, a sociopathic killer.

She'd managed to keep these sorts of thoughts out of her head before. When doubt and unhappiness crept up in the rear of her mind, her passion for her research on killers and her amateur's psychological study of them always canceled depression out. But right now even her interest in Edmund was failing her. In fact, now it was that very thing that was paining her the most. She wanted to be with him, studying him, digging into his brain and heart and soul. Instead she was wandering through the woods with her sister cursing her out.

Why was life so bitterly unfair? There was such a long road of anguish behind her, and now the road before her was punched full of potholes of further suffering. She was setting herself up for failure and knew it, essentially breaking her own heart. What a fool she was to be friends with this murderer, and to tease him with the possibility of something more. But it was just like the girls who fall head over heels for rock stars who are always touring or the girls who spread their legs for movie stars they know they'll never see again. Women had one thing that could get them close to a man who made magic, and they used it, even if for just one night. The lure of men who champion their peers was enough to drive some women mad with desire.

But was Edmund really a champion? He only bested other men when it came to brutality and cruelty. Musicians and artists made magic, but if what Edmund made was magic, it was magic as black as the grave.

Stop it! Lori flinched against her own thoughts. *We all make mistakes. You've made some terrible ones yourself, you stupid bitch. So who are you to judge him?*

Some of the heads he'd ripped from bodies with machetes and axes, the kind of tools she was bound to find in his shack, grim reminders of what he really was. Lori looked to Abby, hoping to take her mind off her mind. Her sister was keeping the pace but her legs were bent further inward now. She was stooped over, breathing through her mouth.

"How're you doing back there?"

"How am I doing what?"

Lori grunted. "I mean are you okay?"

Abby nodded without looking up. She didn't appear interested in conversation. She clearly wanted to keep moving, determined to reach the shack. Lori was starting to have her doubts that they would make it there before sundown, and the thought of wandering around in the woods at night put weight in her chest and an ache to the back of her throat. Even with the flashlights to guide them, the struggle would be greater. They'd be more likely to trip and that could be terrible for Abby. If she took a bad fall, the journey back would be a nightmare. The flashlights could also draw attention. They'd be easier to spot. Thinking of the creepy old man they'd come across, his gospel song echoed through her head. Would he be out here tonight? Would someone else?

They were unnervingly far from civilization. Killen was rural as it was, but now they were into the depths of its unwelcoming wilderness. They hadn't heard so much as a distant airplane, let alone cars or human voices. There hadn't even been motorboats on the river. Not a single fisherman or passing canoe. Even the animals were few and far between now.

Lori stared at the ground and kept on walking, shivering as a river wind rose through the valley. They were alone. Vulnerable. And possibly lost.

Abby's voice was flat. "There it is."

SEVEN

LORI,

Thanks you for them pictures. I know the guards confaskated the good ones that musta showed yer sexy body. The one of just yer face still made me happy in my bed last night. I done cum on it. I gotta be inside you soon. In yer body. In yer mouth. An I will. You can take that shit too the bank.

Im proud of ya fur wantin to proove your love and devotion. You put yourselv above the other girls. Youll go to Killen for me an go to my familys shack. Thats where the key is. Always deep in them woods. I've learned there's only two places a man can find peace—the woods and the grave. I look forward to bein in both. And bein in you. Deep in yer insides. Fuckin you. Hammerin you. Cummin in yer snach and dancin like the ghosts.

Youll believe in what I know. The water be in the valley low. Come see me. Get yer journey. Do this for me an become the one.

Ed

EIGHT

THE SHACK WAS DARK GRAY except for where it was blotched by mold. Vines had crawled up the sides only to die a red death, and a sea of acorns adorned the tin roof and small patch of dirt that served as a yard. There were only two windows, both too small to climb through.

Edmund had not given her a key. The shack was so far out there, it probably didn't even need a lock. There was no one to keep out but the raccoons and possums. Edmund said this was a place even the police hadn't uncovered, that it had been in his family so long there were no state records for it. This was not Edmund's home, but his sanctum.

"The fort," Abby said, cheering up.

They stepped closer. Cobwebs lined the windows, which were cracked and covered in shredded tinfoil on the inside. When Lori reached for the doorknob it turned, but the door had bowed and stuck on the edges. She kicked at the bottom and it gave way. They turned away as a plume of dust rose from the darkness within. There was the odor of rot, as if mice had died somewhere in the walls. She spit against the dirt that found her lips and flicked on the flashlight.

It was a one-room country shack. Pools of standing water

pockmarked the warped floor and the dampness in the cabin was heavy, arctic—far colder than outside. A small wooden table was balanced by rocks beneath the legs. A rusted lantern sat atop the table, along with a metal plate with a black mound on it. An easy chair with the stuffing coming out, molded and yellowed. A wood burning stove thick with soot. Empty whiskey bottles, many shattered. Mounted on the wall hung a painting of Christ, blood pouring from the crown of thorns, his face filled with anguish, eyes white, possessed. The backdrop was solid black, the savior lost in darkness.

Lori swallowed hard. She didn't like it here. Somehow she'd imagined the shack as a quaint cabin, the sort of mountain vacation spot that would be perfect for day trips. There was nothing cozy about this dank pit. It was a place of rot and illness, more mausoleum than home.

Daylight burst in and Lori turned to see Abby tearing the tinfoil from the windows.

"Careful," Lori said. "There may be spiders and broken glass."

"I'm careful."

The natural light made the shack look even worse. The walls were filthy, the ceiling greened by water stains. Lori wanted to get out as soon as possible. If Abby stumbled here, she was likely to get an infection. She tried to remember the last time either of them had received a tetanus shot.

Scanning the area in better light, Lori realized there was no hope chest. No dresser or trunk. She frowned, aggravated, wishing Edmund had given more specific instruction. She went to the table, thinking there might be a drawer in it, and was repulsed by the blackened matter on the plate. Maggots writhed in and out of its tar-like ooze. It could have been food at some point. Maybe it was animal excrement. She didn't want to mess with it to find out. There were no drawers in the table, so she didn't have to get too close.

"I'm hungry," Abby said.

"You don't really wanna eat in here, do you?"

Abby's brow furrowed. "This is the fort, right, Sissy?"

"I didn't know it was gonna be this gross. We shouldn't eat in here, we'll get sick."

Abby looked around the shack, her nose crinkling. There was a sting in Lori's heart when she remembered her sister cursing at her. She hoped this wouldn't become another argument.

"It is yucky," Abby said, much to Lori's relief. "And stinky. It's not like the fort we had."

"No. It's not. We could get sick if we eat in here. We don't want that."

Abby nodded. "Can't be sick. Don't like hospitals."

Lori went to her sister and touched her arm. "Listen, how about you sit outside and have a snack? I need to find something in here. Then we'll have sandwiches together. Okay?"

Abby seemed to mull this over, her mind always one step behind. She was still holding her rabbit's foot and she clutched it close to her chin now, rubbing it along her pale skin. Her eyes were distant, staring into the dark.

"Okay, Sissy."

Lori guided her outside and sat her down on a tree trunk. Abby smiled up at her when Lori opened the backpack and took out a Snickers bar, her favorite.

Relief flowed through Lori, soothing her nerves. Getting Abby out of the shack had quickly become her biggest priority. It was safer out here, and Lori could root through the place quicker if she didn't have to keep checking on her sister. She took off her backpack and placed it near the trunk, taking only the flashlight.

"I'll be just a few minutes," Lori said. "If you need me just shout."

Abby nodded. "'Kay."

Gentle wind blew Lori's hair across her face and she tucked it behind her ears. Looking up, she saw clouds blacker than she'd ever seen before. The sky was an ominous, breathing thing, swollen with rain and threatening to break open. Had the wind been heavier, she'd have feared a tornado. Abby still had her raincoat and hat on. She would be okay if the rain came, and she could always come back into the shack if it got heavy. Hopefully they wouldn't have to wait out a storm inside this rancid hovel.

She crossed the threshold again, the rank stink of death filling her nostrils. She coughed against it, lungs pushing out the dust and rot. The odor seemed stronger now. Something larger than a mouse must have died in here. Perhaps a possum or raccoon had wedged itself beneath the house to die in peace. The thought curdled something in her. Her skin felt tight and greasy as the room's dampness sunk into her flesh.

Where the hell is the chest?

This isn't a goose chase, is it?

She swept through the open space. There was so little of it. Surely she would have spotted a chest if it were in here. Perhaps it was out back. There was no toilet, so there must be some sort of outhouse. Perhaps there was a tool shed too. She turned to go back outside and that's when she noticed a large metal ring on the floor. She turned her flashlight toward it and saw the gaps around the ring, forming a square.

A door.

Lori squatted.

A cellar?

It seemed unlikely for a shack in the woods. Edmund hadn't mentioned one, but he was often vague and prone to leaving things out, as if he enjoyed flustering her with riddles. Staring at the rusted ring, she thought of the trap doors and bottomless pits of the fairy tales Abby enjoyed.

Lori shook the nonsense from her mind. This was just some sort of crawlspace. There would be no swarm of vampire bats to greet her, probably just old junk and firewood. There was nothing to worry about.

And yet she hesitated.

Her neck was cold but sweat was forming at her temples and between her breasts. Her fingers reached then receded, but she wasn't sure what she was really afraid of.

He ripped those women apart.

She shook her head again, forcing her own thoughts away. She was being stupid. There was no way she was going to blow this. She hadn't come all the way out here just to fail. There had been enough failure in Lori's life; she couldn't bear another massive disappointment. Regret had eaten so much of her soul away, beating her down with a depression she marinated in alcohol and weed, using anything to alleviate the pain, even for just a few late hours so she could drift off to sleep. She had a bad feeling about opening this door, but a worse feeling about never having looked inside. What she hadn't done would haunt her, cripple her. Edmund would turn to Niko for his needs and never write to her again. She wouldn't put together a book or do a true crime podcast. She would go back to being a nothing. Back to zero.

Lori grasped the handle, and as the door swung up the stench came with it. She recoiled, gagging and fanning her face. She got down on her knees, turning away from the opening, wishing she'd brought the water bottle in with her so she could swish and spit. If she had she might have overturned the whole thing on her head; she felt that filthy. This hole was like an open grave, earthy and decayed, a septic heap that cradled the warm reek of dying. The air wafting up from it tasted of organic waste and the sound of buzzing insects echoed their frenzy below. Her eyes watered. Pulling her sweater up over her nose, she steadied herself with one hand on the floor and pointed the flashlight into the hole.

You can do this. You have to.

There was a short stairwell. The cellar was cave-like, the walls dirt and rock, lined by wooden buttresses. She tested out the first step. It was sturdy, but even with just one leg in this cramped space

GONE TO SEE THE RIVER MAN

she felt claustrophobic, even though it wasn't one of her common fears. The hallway was so tight it was a wonder Edmund could even fit through it. He would have to take the stairs sideways, and even then it would be a snug fit.

Lori realized she was holding her breath. She let it out and took another step into the abyss. The planks creaked beneath her. Placing her hand on the wall for support, she immediately recoiled from it because of how cold the compressed earth was. The deeper she went, the more potent the stench of decomposition. Something in the air made her eyes burn as if she were cutting onions. She wanted to spit but her mouth was as dry as chalk, her throat warm, raw. The buzzing grew louder, and then the flies were floating around her.

Lori trembled. Every instinct screamed at her to turn back, but still she pressed on, determined to find the chest, determined to win Edmund's gratitude and trust. Her resolve pushed her through dread and disgust and brought her to the last step where the crawlspace turned a sharp left. She pointed the flashlight into the murk.

That's when she saw what she'd been smelling.

Lori instantly turned away to vomit. The regurgitation was forceful but produced little from her empty stomach. She dry-heaved and curled into herself, tears flowing. After retching, she put her hand to her mouth so as not to scream.

It was a dark mass, black with rot and dried blood, more skeleton than flesh. The body was so mutilated she could barely identify it as human. It was the upper torso that gave it away. Despite the rigor mortis and purpled flesh, she could tell the woman had been young. Her black hair was draped with webbing and spiders scurried for cover when the light hit them. The girl's cheeks were hole-punched by maggots, her yellowed teeth exposed beneath. Her breasts had been spread apart, the ribcage pulled open, and what remained of her innards had turned to tarry chunks and ropes of mummified flesh, peppered by flies and their oozing egg sacks. She had been split down the center, from her ribs to her vagina, and was propped up in the corner like a lost doll, one eye socket gleaming in the flashlight's beam, the other filled by gray meat housing a curling worm.

How long has she been down here? Due to public outcry and overwhelming evidence, Edmund's case had been rushed to trial. He had insisted upon it as well. *This must be one of his last victims, a body less than a year old. Being in the cellar must have preserved it longer.*

Lori sobbed in horror. Seeing Edmund's cruelty firsthand brought the reality of it home. It wasn't just a newspaper headline now, not merely stories scrawled on notebook paper in the killer's own hand. It was gruesome, violent death up close—a personal glimpse into a woman's brutal and ultimate end.

What did you expect? He kills people.

He did this. He did this and you're obsessed with him.

Now her own feelings confused her. Was she really obsessed with him and not his actions? She felt kinship and hate for him at the same time, but no hero-worship. She'd just come to feel they were bonded by human pain—her regrets, his depravity. She thought of him as a lost man, almost forgetting he was a monster. No one should have to die the way this young woman had and be left in a hole in the middle of nowhere to become a castle for insects and larvae, her carcass worm-eaten and gutted. Her family didn't know where she had gone. She could have no proper burial and no one who loved her could even have closure.

You should call the police. It's not like Edmund could be in any more trouble. You wouldn't be betraying him. He probably wanted you to see this; after all, he sent you here. And you came, didn't you? You went on his little journey and even brought your poor sister along. How would it have affected Abby if she had seen this? You're such an idiot.

Her thoughts raced, one toppling another, and she ran her hand over her face, trying to control her breathing. When she opened her eyes again, she saw movement, but when she looked directly at the corpse it was still. Her watery vision must have been playing tricks on her, terror giving her mild hallucinations.

The body moved again.

Lori stumbled backward, tripping herself on the bottom stair. She fell on her butt but kept the flashlight pointed at the corpse. Its abdomen was writhing, the black intestines slithering like awakened snakes. Something bubbled and broke, and then a mass wiggled free, chewing and clawing through the remains.

A rat.

The rodent tore its way out only to burrow back into the carcass' mangled groin. Lori got up and turned around, taking the stairs two at a time, her stomach clenching again. She coughed and gagged as she climbed out of the pit. It seemed like the longest set of stairs she'd ever been on. Finally she emerged from the cellar and slammed the door shut behind her, trying not to cry. She didn't want to startle Abby.

Abby.

She wondered if her sister was where she'd left her. Finding the body had filled Lori with paranoia, raw and irrational.

What if this wasn't even Edmund's victim? What if there's another maniac in these woods? She thought of that old man's skeletal grin. *What about Edmund's friend, The River Man? Maybe he and the old man are one in the same.*

Lori called from inside the shack. "Abby?"

"Yeah?"

She exhaled. "Just checking. You doing okay?"

"Yes, Sissy. But I ate my sandwich. I was too hungry to wait. I'm sorry."

"That's okay."

"Are you ready to go?"

Lori remained by the crawlspace door. She'd looked everywhere but hadn't found what she'd been sent here for. She sighed, the weight of another failure driving her down like a railroad spike.

Where else was there to look? She hadn't seen a single . . .

Chest.

The word made the hairs on her body stand up.

They key is in the chest—that's what he said.

She closed her eyes.

No . . .

Lori looked back to the door on the floor.

He couldn't mean . . .

But she knew he did.

NINE

IT WAS LIKE REOPENING A wound. Lori pulled the ring and the cellar door came open, the blackness within pimpling her flesh. She doubted she could do this. Even just going back down there . . .

Her shoulders went tight. She bit at her fingernails. She thought of Edmund and how much he'd come to mean to her in such a short period of time. Had she been swept away too quickly and was now in danger of drowning? She'd always fallen in love too easily. Was her friendship with Edmund much different? Lori always had trouble convincing herself that if something seems too good to be true, it is. She'd thought she'd found something meaningful for the first time in a long time, but had she only been lost in a fantasy that was turning out to be a living nightmare? Did Edmund really want her to prove herself to him this way, or was she just a gullible errand girl?

You're over-thinking again. God, you always do this! Something good happens to you and you're so not used to it you think it has to be some sort of scam. You're so used to life being one big shit that's impossible to flush. Can't you take a chance like you used to? You haven't been with a man since Matt, and you chased him away with your insecurity, clinging to him too much, always needing to know where he was because you were convinced he would leave you for someone else given the opportunity. Well he did leave, but only because you treat-

ed him like some sort of cheater for no reason. You never gave him the trust he deserved.

It's time to believe again. A relationship is nothing without trust.

Lori opened the door.

When she reached the bottom of the stairwell, she had to collect herself before she could turn and face the body again. It was going to take all of her resolve, every bit of nerve she had. With a deep breath she pointed the flashlight at the blackened mass. It writhed with nesting critters. She tried not to look at the dead woman's face, focusing instead on her destination.

You should have brought gloves.

At least there was a tube of hand sanitizer in her pack.

Stay focused on the center of the body. It will seem less human that way. It's just like picking a chicken . . .

But it wasn't. This was not food preparation. This was defiling a corpse. There was a line she was crossing now, no matter how hard she tried to deny it. She was entering Edmund's world in all its putrid violence. That must have been his plan all along, the true meaning of this quest. It wasn't about the key—it was about doing *this* in order to get it. He was not just testing her. He was teaching her about the cold, gruesome reality of what he knew so well, something she longed to comprehend.

This will bring you closer to him.

She was almost surprised to see that as the upshot. And sure, she was doing something forbidden, but it wouldn't be the first time. She certainly hadn't messed around with a corpse before, but she'd engaged in taboos, some so haunting that even years of therapy had failed to ease the mental anguish resulting from those decisions. The shame cloud had never given way to the sunshine of self-forgiveness. So what was one more layer of smoke?

Lori stood over the body, forgetting how to breathe. Rolling up her sleeves, she put the flashlight between her teeth. The best angle would have been to get on one knee, but that would put her down in the girl's decay, so Lori bent over and reached in.

Black globs sluiced between her fingers, turning to liquid at her touch. Lori's stomach churned. She pulled maggot-riddled clumps out of the center of the body's chest, burrowing into it, searching. How big would the key be? One handful at a time, she reached beneath the ribs, into the toxic stew. The body shook as a rodent left it and scurried through the lower dark. Tears welled in the corners of Lori's eyes. They felt suddenly gummy. She was colder than she'd been all day, but that wasn't why she was shaking.

Focus.

Lori kept finding hard things within the sludge, but when she expunged them they were bone fragments, yellow cartilage and other hardened nuggets of carrion. Still she dug, staying busy so the reality of what she was doing wouldn't fully sink in.

Something gleamed, reflecting the light.

Lori dug for it, pulling the hard, flat object until it was firmly in her grasp. Tugging, a webbing of dried flesh came away with it. She ran her fingers over the object, clearing it of human decay. It was a long, old-fashioned key with a round finger hole at the top. She wrung her hands, the excess waste splattering to the floor. She was filthy up to her elbows, but she'd done it. She'd found the damn thing.

Despite it all, Lori smiled.

That's when the cellar door slammed shut.

•••

"Hey!"

Lori's chest went tight. She returned to the staircase and raced up the steps and pushed against the door. It didn't budge. She pushed harder, practically punching the wood. She kicked it, nearly losing her balance. The darkness seemed so much darker now.

"Hey! Hey!"

But she didn't know whom she was calling to, if anybody. Her throat felt as if she'd tried to swallow an apple whole.

Who's here with us?

Has he done something to Abby?

Pounding on the door, she tried to remember if she'd seen a lock on it. All she could remember was the ring handle. Holding in her sobs, she looked around the stairway and shined the light to the cellar floor, searching for something to beat the door with. She had to get out of here and get to Abby. It was time they got the hell away from this place, out of these fucking woods altogether. She hoped it wasn't too late.

She banged on the door again. "Hey! Who's up there?"

This time she got a response. Someone above was laughing. The laughter was deep but light, making it androgynous.

"Abby?"

No answer.

Lori swallowed hard. "Who is that?"

More laughter. It was rising in pitch, sounding childlike.

"Please, let me out of here," Lori cried.

She flinched when the cellar door shook. But it didn't open. Whoever was up there was stomping on the door, maybe even dancing, toying with her.

"Please! Whoever you are, just please . . ."

More dancing. More boyish laughter.

"Somebody help me!"

A voice replied. "Why should I help you?"

Lori stiffened. The voice sounded youthful but somehow familiar. But there was a distortion to it, as if someone were purposely trying to disguise his or her true voice.

"Who is that?" she asked. "Do I know you?"

"In more ways than you should have."

"What? Please, just open this door—"

"What kind of sister are you anyway?"

Lori tensed. Abby had been sitting right outside. Why hadn't she called out for help if a stranger had come to the shack? She was naturally friendly, but surely this secluded place would have put even someone as simple as her on guard.

"Please." Lori struggled with what to say, holding herself against the cold she felt inside and out. "I'm . . . I'm a good sister."

Cruel laughter erupted above, the voice becoming clear and honest. It wasn't a young boy at all, but a female impersonating one. It almost sounded like . . .

"Abby?" Lori said, whispering at first, then growing louder, more assertive. "Abby, is that you?"

The laugh gave her away before she even said, "Hi, Sissy."

Lori sighed with relief, but anger refilled her lungs. She was about to scream at her sister when the cellar door came open, revealing Abby standing there in her forearm crutches, looking down at Lori, a crooked smile on her face. Lori stepped out of the cellar as if being released from a long prison sentence. Even the dilapidated shack looked good after being stuck down in that cave with the body. She slammed the door shut and stood up straight, resisting the urge to smack Abby, wanting to hurt her in the way she hadn't for a long time.

"What were you thinking?" Lori said. "Why would you lock me in there?"

Abby's smile faded. "I . . ."

"I was scared, Abby. Really scared! Why would you want to do that to me?"

"But Sissy, I didn't."

"Didn't what?"

Abby's brow furrowed, figuring out the words. "I didn't lock you in the cellar. It wasn't me."

Lori crossed her arms. "Then who did, Abby? It's just you and me here."

But maybe they weren't alone anymore. Lori looked back and forth, scanning the empty shack. The daylight was even more muted now, allowing the tables and chairs to make shadows that toyed with her nerves. The darkness outside was thickening, alive.

How long was I down there?

"I didn't do it, Sissy. It wasn't me."

"Then who did it?"

"It's not good to be a tattletale." Abby wasn't teasing. She was serious. "Nobody likes a tattle—"

Lori took her sister by the shoulders and shook her.

"Answer me, Abby! If it wasn't you then who was it?"

Abby's face soured, turning pink on its way to purple, the look of a child about to break into a wail. "It was Petey."

Lori released her sister. The mention of her brother's name made her body go slack. She never spoke his name aloud, though she thought about him with painful clarity on an all too regular basis.

"What do you mean it was . . . him?"

Abby's eyes grew wet. "It was Petey. He was mad at you, so he said we should lock you in the cellar down there. It was just a joke."

Lori ran her hand over her head and rubbed at her neck. Closing her eyes to collect herself, she took Abby by the arm. They started walking, Abby leaning on her crutches.

"Where are we going, Sissy?"

But Lori had nothing to say. Abby was acting strange, even for her. She had a head full of dreams but understood fantasy from reality. She wasn't so far damaged she could really think Pete was alive. She'd never had that delusion before. Maybe she was getting worse. Maybe she needed another brain scan. Lori figured it could wait. The important thing right now was she had the key. Edmund was going to be so proud of her.

Abby objected to leaving the shack, but Lori kept walking, dragging her along.

"Sissy, we should wait up for Petey. He said he'd be back."

TEN

LORI COULD HAVE KILLED HER.

Abby had to know how she crushed on David. Lori had been crazy about him all through the school year. Abby was a senior and one of the most popular girls in her class. Boys were always chasing her. Why did she have to go out with the one boy Lori had fallen head-over-heels in love with?

She slammed her locker and crossed her arms, biting her thumbnail as she watched Abby and David chat at the end of the hall. Abby had her back to the wall and he was standing in front of her, bracing himself with his arm stretched out, hand on the wall behind her. Such an intimate stance. Abby was smiling up at him with her pink lipstick and curled lashes, all butterflies and daydreams. Her beauty made Lori want to knock her teeth out.

Sure, she had never told anyone how she felt about David, other than her diary. They had never dated, so it wasn't like Abby had stolen him from her. Still, Lori felt her big sister must have gotten a sense of her attraction to the older boy. She knew Lori better than anyone. David couldn't be expected to know how she felt. Whenever he was around, Lori blushed, fumbled her words and couldn't figure out what to do with her arms, crossing and uncrossing them, putting her hands in her pockets, fussing with her hair. But she had always thought he was friendly to her because he liked her. Liked her in *that way*. Now she realized he'd only been trying to get to her prettier, older sister. Lori had a vision of going home, into Abby's room, and trashing it from top to bottom. She imagined going through her sister's clothes with a pair of scissors and magic markers. Or maybe she would wait until Abby was asleep and give her a little haircut, literally take those dirty blonde locks off her shoulders. What would David think of having a baldy for a girlfriend?

Are they becoming boyfriend and girlfriend?

This was the first time Lori had seen them really flirting, or at least the first time she'd realized it. She wondered if she'd just been naïve, too enamored with David's dreamy eyes and shaggy hair to see the brutal truth when it was right in front of her.

Why would he ever want you?

The question should have come sooner. There was such bitter honesty in it.

You're skinny and don't have Abby's boobs or bottom. You're a dang pancake. Flat and plain. And you're not a senior. You're just a kid to them, a tagalong, a third wheel.

Now she understood that they'd always wanted her gone but had been too nice to say so. It shattered something inside her. She'd never expected anything to come between her and her sister, but now here it stood—a tall, handsome roadblock with wide shoulders and a cute butt.

And yet she still loved David. That's what made it sting so deeply.

Have they been having sex?

Abby had already dated a few guys pretty seriously and had confided in Lori that she'd slept with two of them. Was she fucking David now too? Lori tasted bile at the back of her throat when she thought about it. She gripped the pencil in her hand until it snapped in half and then tossed it to the floor. Her classmates moved past, not even looking at her as they made their escape for the day.

GONE TO SEE THE RIVER MAN

You've never really had a boyfriend. Your first kiss was Adam Sarton. You were twelve and playing spin the bottle with the neighborhood kids, and that turned into seven minutes in heaven in the closet where you let him feel you up. You never spoke to him again. In junior high you went on some dates with Clarence, but he never made a move and neither did you. You didn't even like him all that much; he was just the first guy to ask you to go anywhere. Oh, and then there was Shawn, who cheated on you after one week because you wouldn't let him put his hand up your skirt. You stupid virgin. You basically have no experience with guys. You're clumsy and awkward with everyone. Dang it, Lori, when are you going to stop being a child and become a young woman?

She didn't know the answer to that, but knew it wasn't going to happen unless she made it happen. She was smart enough to understand nothing good came without hard work—her grades, making friends, her summer job at the grocery store. If she wanted a boy in her life, she had to make sacrifices. She had to study if she were to figure out what they wanted, what a boy needs from a girl to make her special to them. And she would do these things, whatever they may be, even if she knew they were wrong.

ELEVEN

DEAREST EDMUND,

So, to answer your questions about my teenage sex life, I guess I'll start by telling you that my parents never gave me the "sex talk." They weren't overly religious or conservative, they just kept sex out of the conversation in our house, and off the TV by limiting our channel access and video rentals. Sex was a secret we kids had to unlock on our own. Abby and I discussed things we heard at school, and sometimes even teased Pete with the latest dirty joke we'd heard in the hallways. Once I'd started my period, I was too embarrassed to even let my parents know. It felt too tied-in to sex. I worried my parents would disown me for simply reaching puberty. Seems ridiculous now, but that's how I felt at the time. But it was time I learned about the changes in my body and hormones, so I read about sex and procreation in biology books in the library. I've always been a bookworm (one day I even hope to write one). You see, I was kind of a wallflower and escaping into studies and the worlds within novels helped me to cope with my loneliness. I never looked into pornography. Nowadays you can find free porn with a click of a mouse, but back then you had to be an adult to get those dirty movies and magazines. I would have been curious, for sure,

GONE TO SEE THE RIVER MAN

but pornography was unavailable to me.

Not that I would've used porn for its intended purpose. At the time, I thought masturbation was a shameful thing. Most of those dirty jokes I heard at school were about it, particularly of boys doing it, and what losers they were for not being able to make it with a real girl. I could never touch myself back then, especially not under my parents' roof. It would break my mother's heart. Dad would kick me out on the streets. I just knew it. It's funny how inadvertently parents can warp a child's sexuality in ways that extend far into their adulthood. Perhaps if sex wasn't such a taboo subject, if an unspoken rule about it hadn't been imposed by such silence, my early experiences with sex wouldn't have been so scarring and demented, if that's the right word. Without intending to, my parents gave me the impression that sex *was* demented, that there was no getting around it being filthy and degrading and wrong. My siblings experienced a similar mental crippling on the matter. Their actions make it hard for me to think otherwise.

The first time I actually saw people having sex, I was still a virgin. I was just fifteen. It was early fall and I decided to take a walk in the woods. I love that time of year and always enjoyed going for hikes while listening to my Walkman, playing bands like The Cure, Tori Amos and The Smashing Pumpkins (what were your favorites growing up?). I could zone out and escape into my own little world. I could imagine myself as a rock star, playing for a crowd full of my classmates, gaining the attention and popularity I so desperately wanted while expressing my deepest emotions through a voice that would give people goose pimples.

Anyway, there was a special spot deep in the forest behind my parents' house where my sister and I built a swing over a stream. We swam there in the summer, and when fall came we would just hang out on the cliff. That day I was going down there to write in my diary about something that was really tearing me up (that's why I'd brought cassettes by bands that sang really sad songs). See, my older sister had fallen for the same boy I had fallen for, but she was older and prettier and basically better than me in every way, so she won him and became his girlfriend. Not that it was ever a contest. I never even tried to get this boy—his name was David. He was out of my league but I just couldn't help obsessing over him, you know? I'm sure you've felt that way before too, a sort of helpless longing for someone that becomes a runaway train in your head. So I was really torn up over David and Abby being together. And now he was over at our house a lot and the two of them would sit on the couch, her cradled in the nook of his arm while they watched *The Simpsons* and *Seinfeld*, snuggling closer with each laugh. I would go to my room just to not have to see them happy together. Well, he happened to be over this particular afternoon, but he and Abby had left to go to the arcade before I headed to the trails.

When I got to the special place by the creek, there was a young couple on a throw blanket by the edge of the cliff. The boy was above the girl and she had her legs wrapped around him. She wore a pink sweater but was nude from the waist down. The boy still had his jeans on, but they were down around his knees. He was thrusting in and out of her and they were kissing. Before I got a close look at them, I ducked behind some shrubs, embarrassed by the situation. I didn't want them to see me, but at the same time I was too curious to walk away. What I'd seen in that moment excited me. This was a chance to have a mystery solved. I craved some sort of experience because I knew this was what boys would expect of me. Maybe by watching what this girl did, I would be good at sex when I finally had it, or at least better than I would have without a demonstration.

So I poked my head out just far enough to see them, and when they stopped kissing, I recognized my sister's flushed face. David was making love to her. They were breathing heavy with these quiet little moans, each one a new nail in my heart. That's when I realized that—despite them being a couple—I had retained some semblance of hope that one day David would turn around and realize I loved him more than Abby ever could. I had a small amount of faith in that, even if I'd never really admitted it to myself. Seeing them making love ruined that delusion. It took it all away, including my romantic fantasies, the thoughts of David that came when I listened to love songs or read romantic books. I couldn't even have magic moments with him in my head now. All I would see was David having sex with my sister, making her moan and sweat and turn as pink as her sweater.

I must admit I grew teary-eyed. But still I watched them, right until the end when David shuddered in his orgasm. I got lower in the bushes when he climbed off of her, sneaking a peak at his penis. It was still hard. I'd never seen an erect one before, only illustrations in human anatomy books. It was disturbing to my virgin eyes—ugly, veined, wet.

The two of them redressed but stayed on the blanket, kissing and cuddling. They were so casual about what they'd just done; I could tell it wasn't their first time together. Somehow that made it all worse. I told myself I could never forgive David, but knew it wasn't true. The one I could never forgive was *Abby*. I told myself I had no sister now. I felt a rage toward her unlike anything I'd ever felt against another person, not even for Tammy Holliston and her mean friends who'd bullied and tormented me all through junior high. It was not just jealousy that made me loathe my sister. That was part of it, but not the worst part. I felt betrayed by the one person I trusted most. I'd always looked up to Abby. She was everything I wanted to be. Now she'd shown her true colors. My own sister was a snake in the grass and I'd been duped by her loving sibling act. I'd never felt so foolish. It hurt.

Of course, in time, I forgave Abby. She's my sister and I love her and take care of her now. But for this moment in time I had a silent anger that hurt so bad I couldn't even confront her with it. My thoughts of revenge were my own private poison and it began to rot me from the inside out. That's when everything really started to change for me.

I've never told anyone else about catching Abby with David. You're special to me, Edmund. Maybe David could have been too, if he had chosen me. Things would've been so different if he had. I believe, very deeply, that everything that happened after that day would never have gone down had it not been for me seeing what I saw.

More on that in my next letter. Right now I have to take Abby for a follow up with her doctor, and then I have to get to the diner. I'm working late tonight, but hopefully we can talk on the phone soon. I've enclosed some money so you can ring me.

Yours,
Lori

TWELVE

THE SKY DIDN'T LOOK RIGHT. The storm produced clouds that moved too quickly, the firmament as alive as the churning river below, and distant thunder rumbled like a strummed guitar, serenading their hike with gloomy ballads. They were along the shore but stuck to the hard earth so Abby's crutches wouldn't sink in the sand. Mist rose from the murky waters, the current splashing froth across every cluster of black rock.

Lori stared into the valley. Towering trees swayed with vibrant, red leaves and the river reflected their hue. Her thoughts had drifted to her childhood and she bit at her lip, hoping physical pain would block out the trauma. Behind her, Abby was breathing heavy, but had mercifully kept silent. After her little stunt back at the shack, Lori didn't have the patience for her babbling.

Petey. She'd said it was Petey.

Something wasn't right with Abby. Today there was darkness to her weirdness. Had her brain damage given way to psychotic delusion? Would she become a danger to herself? To others? It was hard to imagine Abby being a threat to anyone. She'd always been a gentle soul, before and after the accident. That's what made her mean prank so unsettling. It wasn't like her at all. Just like the *fuck you*.

A trail appeared on their left, winding over the next hill like a rattlesnake's skin. The shoreline was getting closer to the terrain. It was best to veer back into the woods. Lori started toward the trail and felt a deeper chill on the stagnant air. The scent of decayed leaves and wet bark rose from the ground with each footstep. It was dead silent here. Not even the chirping of birds or insects. Only the river—an ever-flowing monster that cleaved the valley in two.

"This way," she said.

Her sister moaned. "I'm tired, Sissy."

Lori looked back at her. Abby was leaning heavily on the forearm crutches, her shoulders high and tight, head hung between them. Pain contorted her face. Her legs were bowed and bent at the knees, dangling like dead appendages. At one time they'd been completely paralyzed. It was a wonder she could move as much as she could. Right now, her stilted walking was a grim reminder of things Lori wanted to forget.

"I'm tired too," Lori said. "I just want to get where we're going so we can finish this."

While in the cellar, she'd been struck by a terror so thick she wanted to completely abort the mission to find The River Man and head back to the car as quickly as they could. But once they'd left the shack she'd had yet another change of heart. Part of it was a desire to uncover the mystery Edmund had offered to her. It was a once in a lifetime thing. But another part of it was that Lori was fickle and hated herself for it. She'd always done better having someone else make her decisions for her. She preferred to be led. Edmund wanted her to do this, and so she would. There was no way she could turn back now, not after digging into a corpse for the sake of the quest.

"Sissy, I don't think we should be here."

"What do you mean?"

But Abby wouldn't say. She was staring at the ground, cautious of every step, always afraid of hurting her legs again. The terrain was getting more difficult too, with thick roots and jutting rocks. The

GONE TO SEE THE RIVER MAN

trail smoothed out ahead, but it was a steep hill to climb. Lori wondered just how far she could push her crippled sister. She certainly didn't want to leave Abby behind to wait for her to finish this journey. Lori was bound to lose her in these woods. But there was no way of knowing when this search would even end. From Edmund's childlike map, she'd assumed getting to the shack wouldn't take half as long as it had. Now she was facing the possibility that finding The River Man could take days. She'd hoped to be in and out before sundown, but dusk was already making itself known, even through the filtered light of the rainy day.

She was about to call for a snack break when a voice jolted her.

"Who in the hell's that?" the man shouted.

Lori looked up. At the crest of the hill was a shadowy figure, stocky and thick. His arms were raised, holding something, pointing it at them. Lori got in front of Abby. She said nothing.

"What the hell y'all doin' up 'round here?" The man took a few steps down the path, the shotgun now in full view but his face remaining in shadow. "Ain't y'all know this here be private property?"

Lori shook her head. "We're sorry . . ."

The man moved closer. Lori had to resist the urge to run. Abby would never be able to keep up with her. Besides, the man may very well pump his shells into their backs. She put up her hands in a passive, apologetic manner.

The guy looked country as dirt. A black man in his sixties—big belly, gray and balding head, stained jeans held up by suspenders. To her surprise, he wasn't giving them the evil eye. Instead he looked pensive, curious. Seeing they were not a threat, he lowered his weapon.

"Shiiiit," he said in a slow drawl. He had few teeth, all of them yellowed and crooked. But his face was kind, almost grandfatherly. "Y'all lost or somethin'?"

Lori wasn't sure what to tell him. He seemed friendly enough, but was still a large man holding a double-barrel shotgun. She thought of the bear mace in her pack.

"Just passing through," she said.

"Passin' through to get to what? Ain't nothin' down this here river. Current's too strong to do no wadin' or swimmin'. Y'all get pulled in an drown if'n ya try that. Some days I can't even take the fishin' boat out."

Lori nodded but had no words.

"Well then, what in blazes ya be up in here for, girl?"

Unable to come up with a convincing lie, she decided to come clean. Maybe the old man could even help her find the person she was looking for.

"I've come to see The River Man."

The man's face sank, his warmth fading to a somber cold. He shook his head. "Lady, you be talkin' crazy."

"Do you know where I can find this man?"

"Whatchu wanna find him for?"

"I was asked to find him."

"By who?"

"Just a friend."

The man blew out a silent whistle. "Your friend musn't be right in the head."

"What do you mean?"

Thunder moaned above them, a storm coming closer, mile by mile. The old man looked skyward, holding the shotgun with one hand, his grip loose, unthreatening. Lori was tempted to make a grab for it, just in case, but didn't have the nerve.

"Rain ain't done with us noways." The thunder's moan turned to a roar, backing him up. "Imma get inside. Y'all can come on up if'n ya want to. Ya wanna keep passin' through, that'd be fine too. Just stay away from my chicken coop. They spook easy."

Lori looked to Abby but she was still staring at her feet. Exhaustion had deflated her and she showed no interest in this stranger. Even if they turned back now, there was no way they were getting out of these woods by nightfall, and rain was about to rip apart the sky.

"I'm Lori," she said, extending her hand, praying he wouldn't grab hold of her, that this wasn't a terrible mistake.

He shook it gently. "Name's Buzz."

"Hello, Mr. Buzz."

"Nah, nah. It's Mr. Fledderjohn. Junior Fledderjohn. But they done called me Buzz some fitty years now. Come on up for a spell. Don't wanna be out in this weather."

"Where's your place?"

"Just over this here hill yonder. Gonna makes me some supper. Y'all can join me."

Lori looked to Abby again. Her sister hadn't moved. She was incredibly still and pale.

There was no choice.

•••

The shack was twice as large as Edmund's but still a small living space. It had begun to rain and the drops clacked on the tin roof like firecrackers. A wall of chicken wire surrounded Buzz's coop, a weathercock spun atop it, squealing for oil. There was a dilapidated dog house but no dog in sight, and the porch was equally deteriorated with a rusted auger, broken bicycle and moldy cable spools taking up a good deal of space. To one side, a stack of firewood as high as the shack itself made the floorboards bow. A generator was chained to a tree. If there was a yard, it was smothered by fallen leaves.

"Don't mind my mess," Buzz said. "Weren't spectin' no company."

When he pushed the door open a huge Saint Bernard burst forth, causing Lori to step back. But like his owner, the dog was friendly and came to the sisters at once, licking and sniffing at their hands.

"It's a dog, Sissy." Abby was coming back to life a little. She petted the dog excitedly. "He's a good dog, Sissy."

"That there's Jo-Jo," Buzz chuckled. "He loves most everybody."

Lori smiled but didn't pet Jo-Jo. She was still a little on edge, especially now that they were going inside. Even though they were no safer in the woods, being so far from civilization, going into the man's home seemed so much riskier. She tried not to think of being tied and bound in a cellar like Edmund's, and it pained her to realize her own hypocrisy. The man she considered a friend, a man she thought of constantly, almost fondly, had actually done to women the exact thing she was now worried about.

Buzz's shack was also one room. Tables, a wood burning stove, a twin bed in the corner, a dog bed beside it, nearly as big. An old tube radio on a TV stand, a record player next to it. A painting of ducks on a pond, the frame lined with dust. A black and white photo of a young, African-American woman with starry eyes and a smile like magic. An urn beside it. In one corner was a coat rack with a worn fedora on a rung, two fishing poles beside it. In the other corner, an acoustic guitar on a stand. Buzz put the shotgun on the floor by the poles, propping it against the wall, then walked away without a care. Lori could easily grab it. Buzz didn't seem worried at all. His trust began to rub off on her, her muscles relaxing as she helped Abby to the flower-patterned couch. Buzz sat in a stained recliner and started rocking.

"Just gotta sit a spell before cookin'," he said. "Done got old. Gettin' up dat hill ain't easy like it useta done be." He looked at Abby. "Reckon it's even harder for you, girl."

Abby lied back and slid her arms out of her crutches. She reached for a blanket. Dog hair drifted into the air when she moved it, and she turned on her side, sighing.

"It's been a long day," Lori explained.

"Musta been. Y'all are pretty deep in. Carport's many miles out, 'less ya'll came by boat."

"No. We parked at the edge of the woods where the trail begins. We've been walking all day."

Buzz shook his head. "All because your friend done telled ya to?"

Lori shrugged. "I didn't think it'd be all that difficult."

"*Difficult?* Ya gone to see The River Man, and ya think it ain't gonna be difficult?"

Another shrug. "I don't know what I thought."

"Ya must really like this ol' friend a yours to go doin' somethin' like this here. These woods—they ain't so friendly."

"Oh?"

"Mmm-hmm. Believe that."

She tried to smile but it didn't come naturally. "You seem friendly. Jo-Jo too."

"Well, much obliged. But we be the exception. These woods . . ."

He trailed off. Having heard his name, Jo-Jo came over and sat between them, huge and slobbery. The rain was falling harder now, making the roof crackle and pop. A carefully positioned array of pots and pans caught the water that trickled through.

"But you live out here," Lori said. "There must be something you like about it."

Buzz leaned back, folded his hands. "The Fledderjohns done been in Killen a lotta years. Use ta live on the other side of the river, in a cabin not much bigger than this. That's where I was born, right inside that cabin. See, Daddy didn't like nobody after the war. Wanted us to live deep in these woods, so that's what we done did. I was raised on this here river and woulda never left if it ain't been for my Hattie." He pointed to the urn and the photo beside it.

"Your wife?"

"Ah, yeah. My sweet lil' Hattie. Met her in town, ya know. I was working at the steel mill and useta eat lunch at the diner she done worked at. When we fell in love, she told me all she'd ever wanted was to get on outta this place. So I gots me a new job up in Canton, and we got married and had us a family there. Once she was dead and gone and the kids done moved away, I couldn't stand to be in the house alone no more. It all just reminded me of her too much. So I came on back home to Killen. Guess in a way I always knew I would. Nobody leaves this river for long. Believe that."

Buzz reached to the end table beside him and opened a cigar box. Instead of a stogie he pulled out a Mail Pouch sack and tucked a pinch of tobacco under his lip. He was looking out the window, through the tree branches and falling rain, out into the woods, as if seeing something far gone though never forgotten. He was a talkative man, and Lori felt she could use his loneliness to keep him chatting, maybe unearth whatever he knew about this river and the man named after it.

"Why do you say that?" Lori asked. "About no one leaving the river?"

"Cuz ain't nobody does."

Buzz spit into a can of Pabst that had its lid peeled off. Beside Lori, Abby snored softly, the purrs of a cat. There were dark rings under her eyes and her flesh was ghostly, face sunken. Lori patted her sister's head, brushed back her hair.

"So," Lori said to Buzz, "you seem to know who I'm talking about."

Buzz looked back at her but said nothing.

"I just need to see this River Man, whoever he is, so I can—"

"So you can deliver somethin' to him, yeah. I know it."

Lori paused. "Yes. That's right."

"Shit. Course ya doin that. Lord, how they come and go."

"Who?"

Buzz leaned forward. "Y'all ain't the only folks to come down this here river searchin' for him. They always come with some lil' thing, like a token for a toll. River Man always need one."

"I don't understand."

GONE TO SEE THE RIVER MAN

Buzz's brow fell, eyes turning to flint. "And best you shouldna. You and your sista oughta take whatevers you got for him and just toss it in the damned river. Get outta these woods before ya get into trouble."

A tingle hit the back of Lori's neck. "What are you telling me?"

"I'm tellin' you . . ." Buzz rubbed the gray scruff on his chin, searching for the right words. "There's history in these here woods, and history to the ol' River Man too. Mama thought Daddy was crazy for wantin' to live out here, based on all she knowed 'bout Killen. But Daddy didn't take no backtalk from her or nobody. There was somethin' in his blood that done drew him to this place, this river.

"See, back when I was a-growin' up, all us kids who done lived in the river shacks, we all useta scare each other talkin' 'bout The River Man. He was, like, a ghost story. I dunno where the story started, and don't remember ever *not* knowin' it. But it goes like this here. Ya know them old stories about a bluesman sellin' his soul to the devil to be the best guitar player in the world?" Lori nodded and Buzz continued. "That's what they said about Robert Johnson—that sold off his soul to the Prince of Darkness down in Mississippi. Lotsa songs about sellin' ya soul to Satan, lotsa stories. River Man was a story like that, only he didn't make no deal with the devil. People along this river make deals with The River Man, deals like the one Robert Johnson made with Satan."

Buzz spat into his beer can. His weathered face was a canyon carved by hardship, the lines deep enough to hold a dime in. Darkness was settling in now. He reached for the oil lantern at his feet, brought it to the table and lit it. The shack flickered an orange glow like the inside of a jack-o-lantern.

"River Man ain't wantin' nobody's soul. What he wants is for your soul to be *as bad as his*. Ya get what ya want without havin' to do anythin' for him, but somehow he just brings out the worst in ya. Ya go rotten in your heart after dealin' with The River Man. That's what I growed up believin'. Everybody knew somebody that done made a deal with him, and they got their wish but ended up doin' terrible things too; not because they owed it to him, but because he sorta, ya know, *inspired* them."

Lori crossed her arms. She hadn't been prepared for mountain folk superstitions. She'd expected The River Man to be a mere nickname. Now she felt like she was literally chasing a ghost.

"What kind of terrible things?" she asked.

"Shit . . . settin' fires. Robbery. Murder. All kinds a stories 'bout mamas poisonin' their babies an tossin' 'em in the river. Men rapin' and cuttin' up lil' girls. Them stories been told 'round these here parts forever and a day. That's 'cause this land's been home to so much blood. It's cursed earth."

"Really?"

"Aw, shit yeah. Goin' back to when it was first settled. The original name of this here place was Killing. That's how bad it was. That's why ain't nobody wanna live out here. They changed the name to Killen, but that shit don't help none. Only folks on this river are those sorry nuff to be born here. We just can't shake it loose."

Buzz settled back into his chair and shifted the dip in his mouth. Lori put her elbows on her knees, inching closer, wanting more answers.

"You think this River Man is real?"

Buzz seemed to mull this over. "Depends on what day ya ask me. Months can go by an everythin's peaceful in these woods. River's like a sleepin' baby. Makes me think that River Man is just tall tales. But then somethin' awful happens and that fear I felt as a lil' un comes a-creepin' on back. I lived here all my life and I ain't never seen The River Man. I know it's gotta be just tall stories. I'm a grown man and don't wanna believe. But I'm old enough now to know there are some things nobody can ever really unnerstand. Folks believe in God. They believe in the Devil. Why not The River

GONE TO SEE THE RIVER MAN

Man? Somethin's gotta make people wanna kill each other. Somethin's gotta make a soul go bad enough to make somebody rape 'n' murder. Ya can call it whatever ya wanna, but 'round here it's always been him, always The River Man."

Lori nodded. "But is he a real person, like, flesh and blood?"

"Reckon the only folks who know that are the fools who done go to him. Gotta be invited to The River Man, just like your friend invited you. That's how it works—like a chain letter, like dominoes. One person gets what all they want from him, and then they send him someone else to make a deal with. Looks like your friend done chose you."

Lori closed her eyes. Her fingertips had gone numb. It was full dark now. Night had come upon them almost without notice and it made her feel smaller somehow, weaker.

"And the trinket?" she asked.

"That's how The River Man knows you're for real. When you get sent to him, ya can't come empty handed. Ya bring him somethin' special, somethin' that proves ya got what it takes to uphold your part of the deal. Most times it ain't really what ya got, but how ya got it."

The rotting carcass oozed through Lori's mind and she winced it away. "This all seems crazy to me. I mean, why would my friend send me out to chase some Grimm fairy tale? It doesn't make sense."

"Well, shit, that's what I thought when ya done told me. Told ya your friend must be crazy, didn't I? Who are they anyway?"

Lori wondered if Buzz would recognize the name or if these hillside hermits never spoke to one another. Edmund said the shack had been in the Cox family for generations, and Buzz had lived out here most of his life. It seemed likely he would know who Edmund was and be familiar with the horrible things he'd done, some right along this river.

"His name's Eddie," she said, telling a half-truth. This was not a nickname Edmund had ever used.

Buzz's eyes flashed with recognition anyway. His mouth fell agape, the sludge within threatening to spill out like black vomit. "Only one Ed ever been up 'round here. And I sure as hell hope he ain't your friend."

She should have lied. She knew that. But in a way she'd wanted Buzz to know. It was almost impossible for her not to brag about her special kinship with a celebrity of sorts. She could only hope Buzz wouldn't kick them out into the cold rain for associating with the local serial killer.

"Tell me ya don't mean Edmund Cox," he said.

She hesitated before admitting it. Lori had never seen a black person go pale before. Buzz's face was suddenly ashen, as if he were lying in his coffin, shocked at his own death. With some difficulty, he stood up from his chair and went to the window, leaning on the sill. He spat out his wad of dip into a spittoon by the coat rack.

"How?" he asked.

"How what?"

"How could anybody be friends with a sum bitch like that? Ya gotta know what all he done did."

Lori sighed. "I do."

"And still ya call him friend?"

She paused. "Yes. He is . . . a friend."

"He's Sissy's special friend," Abby said. She turned over on the couch, her bleary eyes fluttering. "She's gonna marry him someday and I get to be the bestest maid."

Buzz turned around, facing the sisters. Lori was sure he was going to tell them to get the hell out of his house and never come back. Instead he just shook his head, his face flickering with bewilderment as he went to the kitchen. He opened a cabinet and took out a bottle.

"Need Wild Irish Rose to get my head 'round this."

Buzz removed the cap and took a swig straight from the bottle.

GONE TO SEE THE RIVER MAN

He opened a box, retrieved a container and put it on the counter. Sudden revulsion twisted Lori's innards, imagining Buzz keeping some sort of grisly evidence of Edmund's crimes in the Tupperware. She exhaled when she saw it was only a corn dish.

"Guess we oughta eat," he muttered.

Lori went to him. Buzz noticeably backed away.

"Sorry to upset you," she said, not knowing how to explain. "But really, I'm not going to marry him. Abby just likes to tease me. It's just that—"

"Makes sense. Cox goin' to see The River Man. He did just the kind of thing ya do after ya go an make a deal with him. Ain't the first man to murder folk in Killen, but he gots to be one-a the worst. Lord, how they come and go."

"You keep saying that. What do you mean by 'how they come and go'?"

Buzz dumped the hominy into a small pot. "Y'all ain't the first ladies to come to this place 'cause some bad man told 'em to. Same thing happened to my poor lil' mama. If'n a man has wickedness in his blood, he gonna find The River Man, and he gonna take the woman he loves with him."

A warm rush surprised Lori. *The woman he loves...*

Abby was snoring on the sofa again. Lori chose not to wake her for food just yet. Buzz put eggs into one pan and took bacon from a wrapping of butcher paper. Her stomach groaned as the food sizzled. She was suddenly starving, the journey having emptied her.

"Does he have a name? The River Man?"

"Nah, just go by The River Man."

"And your father?" Lori forced herself to ask. "Did he go looking for The River Man too?"

Buzz stared down into the pans as if searching his own eyes in a mirror. Lori wondered if she'd asked one question too many.

"Yeah," was all he said.

Lori let it be.

THIRTEEN

THERE WAS NO WAY SHE could muster the nerve to ask a boy to have sex with her.

Lori was far too shy and totally insecure about everything relating to sex. That was why she had to lose her virginity now, even though the thought made her nauseous with dread. She needed experience if she was ever going to be good at sex, and if she were ever going to get a boyfriend, she would have to learn how to do it right. That's what boys wanted. Even sweet boys like David.

Sitting on her bed, legs hugged close to her chest, Lori watched the rain trickle down the window that looked out into the yard. The afternoon storms came regular in the summertime. It was one of the few things she liked about this time of year. Summer was all too good at reminding her what a loser she was. She didn't get to go tubing like other teens or go to late night gatherings where garage bands played live and alcohol somehow got snuck in. She had few friends, all of them nerds like her, girls as plain as white bread with warm milk, the kind who favored working on the school yearbook to partying at the lake. Lori wanted to be one of those older girls who wore bikini tops and cut-off shorts and held on to boys while they rode on dirt bikes. She wanted to be cool with a cigarette in her mouth, sexy in a jean skirt. But this was something she couldn't

GONE TO SEE THE RIVER MAN

force. She couldn't will her desires into existence. It was going to take work. Everything always did.

She closed her diary, finally out of words for her pain. She was so awkward, so unpopular, so danged alone. No one could understand. Not her parents, not Abby, not Pete. Not her stupid, lame friends. She never even tried to explain what she was going through. She kept her inner hell private. Confiding in others would only add more flames. You couldn't trust people. Abby taught her that by taking David away from her. Abby *took*. She didn't ask for things she wanted; she snatched them out of the air like she was scooping a butterfly in a net. She dominated life without trying. While Lori got things through hard work, her big sister seemed to get everything she wanted through a sort of whimsical, carefree romp, spinning like gold in the sunshine of her perfect, pretty life. Things came to her effortlessly—beauty, popularity, boys. Lori had never been able to just *take*.

Maybe that was her problem.

Maybe that's what she had to change.

•••

Having climbed over the windowsill, Abby tiptoed on the carpet of her bedroom and slowly closed the window so not to wake anyone. It was a colder than normal night in September and she'd wished she'd brought a jacket. At least she was home now and could climb under the blankets.

It was past two in the morning. If her parents knew she'd snuck out to a party she'd been invited to at a college campus, she'd be grounded and wouldn't be eligible for parole until she was forty. Frat parties meant sex, and in this house, sex was a capital offense. Abby had only once tried to talk to her parents about it, and they shut the conversation down immediately, giving her orders to simply not do it, that she was too young to even be thinking about it. It made her feel so ashamed that she hadn't brought any boys around until David, who came off as so sweet and harmless Mom and Dad would never expect how horny he was.

There had been a lot of boys at the party. And to make matters worse, she was a little tipsy. She couldn't hide that sort of thing from Mom. As stoic as he was, Dad was easier to push over. She'd bat her eyes, be his sweet little girl again, and she'd be off the hook for most things. But Mom could be a real battle-ax. In this house, she was the law, especially over her daughters. Pete was the only one who could melt her. Always had been. When Abby was younger, she'd resented him for that, thinking he was Mommy's favorite. Now that she was a teenager, she had come to understand the dynamics of her family's relationships a little better, and her envy had subsided. Pete was Mom's little boy, just as Abby was Daddy's little girl. And Dad was tougher on his son than either of his daughters, even though Pete was the youngest. He seemed to expect more from his son. It made Abby feel somewhat neglected. It confused her to want more pressure from him, seeing how Mom gave her more than she could handle sometimes.

She kicked out of her Converse, took off her blouse and wiggled out of her too-tight stonewashed jeans. She'd always been the type to change into her pajamas the moment she got home, even if she had no intention of going to bed. She was beat now though. She didn't even want to bother brushing her teeth. The mattress before her was too inviting to be delayed . . . but she had to pee. Beer went through her in a storm. She'd only had three, but her bladder was swollen like a ham. Though nervous about waking her parents, she figured there was nothing suspicious about her taking a late-night pee. They wouldn't get out of bed just for that.

Out in the hall, Abby squinted in the dark, waiting for her eyes to adjust. She braced herself against the wall to guide her in her blindness, still tiptoeing just in case. Better to be silent than get busted with a buzz. It was her attention to that silence that made the sounds from Pete's room noticeable. They were soft and low, muted behind the door. She figured they were just his regular sleep

GONE TO SEE THE RIVER MAN

noises. He often mumbled gibberish when he was asleep, especially when he was having night terrors. Abby moved on toward the bathroom, passing in front of Pete's door. As always, it was slightly ajar because it didn't fit properly into the frame. Dad had been talking about sanding it down for so long now it had become a family joke. The noises became clearer as she approached. Pete was moaning, breathing in short bursts.

Abby stopped.

Pete's night terrors were sometimes so bad he walked in his sleep, stumbling down the hall to escape whatever imaginary threat was chasing him. Once he had fallen down the stairs that way, which was why the gate had been placed at the foot of the stairs, to keep him from breaking his leg again. If he was having a nightmare bad enough to make him breathe heavy and groan like this, it was probably best to wake him, but she had to do it slowly, gently, so he wouldn't snap awake with a scream and wake the whole damned house. Abby took the doorknob, pushing the door open without so much as a whisper on the carpet.

At first, she thought she'd entered Lori's room by mistake. Abby's sister was wearing nothing but a bra, her small body glowing blue in the light of the moon as she moved back and forth on the bed, like she was riding a horse. The heavy breathing was actually hers, but the moans were Pete's. The hairs on Abby's arms rose up when she spotted her brother in the shadows. He was beneath Lori, naked, and she was on his lap, moving up and down.

Abby put her hand over her mouth, a gag holding in a scream. The booze in her head dropped back down to her stomach. Her body trembled as she turned away, wanting to burn the image from her mind's eye, wanting to erase the night entirely. Trotting to the bathroom quickly and quietly, Abby raised the toilet seat.

She would have to brush her teeth after all.

•••

Days before Abby caught them, Pete was in the shower. He was taking longer ones now that he'd hit puberty. Discovering masturbation had changed his life, ending the constant wet dreams that left his groin sticky every morning. Doing this also lessened the spontaneous erections he got at school, ones so obvious he had to carry his books in front of his crotch so no one would see. There were some girls so attractive that all they'd have to do was glance at him and his pecker would turn to granite. He thought of them during his long showers, his penis soaped up, legs trembling.

There was a sudden noise. Pete spun in the shower, facing the curtain. Shame and horror struck him like a baseball bat when he saw the blurred shape open the door and softly close it behind them, a shape too small to be Dad. That only left . . .

"Hey!" he said, annoyance mixing with fear of being caught. "Can't you see I'm in here?"

He hoped it wasn't Mom. He never would have talked to her that way. The person behind the curtain didn't say anything, but moved closer, revealing their identity.

"Lori?" he said. "Get out of here! I'm in the shower!"

The curtain came back so fast Pete didn't have time to put his hands in front of his genitals. Lori stood there, face slack, eyes going right to his erection. Pete spun around, flesh prickling, mouth going tight.

"What're you doing?" Pete asked.

He was tempted to scream for his parents, to get Lori in trouble or at least get her the hell out of the bathroom. But he didn't. Long ago, it had been instilled in him not to rat on his sisters, to never be a little snitch. That was how he'd been accepted into the circle the three siblings had formed. It was a lesson he'd never forgotten, and it kept him quiet now, even as the needles of panic began to prick.

"You better get outta here," he said.

Lori stared at his backside. "I know what you're doing."

He looked his sister in the eye at first, then his gaze lowered. Last year, he'd peeped on Abby while she was changing. It was a habit he grew out of, but sneaking glances at her by hiding in her closet had given him his first erection. The last time he peeped her, he had masturbated while watching her change clothes, coming within seconds, and had felt so ashamed afterward that he never peeped on her again. He'd never peeped on Lori, but he couldn't help but notice she was developing now too. She had small boobs and a curve to her hips that hadn't been there before.

Noting his wandering gaze, Lori smiled at him, but it was a different kind of smile, warped, somewhat macabre.

"Can I watch?" she asked.

FOURTEEN

LORI SNAPPED AWAKE, HER HEART high in her throat, lodged there. She didn't know where she was. It was dark here and smelled of animals and rain. Reaching out, her hand hit a hard floor. Something snorted next to her, and she gasped as a huge tongue wet her face. She shooed the dog away as yesterday came back to her: the journey through the woods, accepting Buzz's invitation to stay and . . .

. . . the body in the cellar . . . the key for The River Man.

A loud snore startled her. She turned over to see the silhouette of Buzz passed out in his chair. He'd given Lori his bed, Abby the couch—a true gentleman. Even after she'd confessed her friendship with Edmund Cox, Buzz hadn't tossed them out. He had to be desperately lonely. Lori couldn't imagine living in these woods with no TV or internet, no neighbors, no running water, the only electricity provided by gasoline. No one to talk to but a big, drooling mutt. Isolation like that would be too reflective, an introspective solitude impossible for her to endure. The past needed to stay buried, not repeatedly unearthed by a troubled mind with no distractions.

She wondered what time it was. Looking out the window, she saw a faint, gray glow creeping out from behind the tree line. Dawn wasn't here, but it would be within the hour, and the earlier they got started the sooner it would all be over. She could put Buzz's ghost stories to rest and reach the actual man she'd been sent here to meet. Hopefully the handing over of the key would be quick and easy. She wanted to just get it over with; not only to put an end to this trek up river, but also to prove herself worthy to Edmund once and for all. It was a need that had grown inexplicably stronger, making her question her motives. Since the trip had begun, she'd been yearning to complete this task, no longer to just gain access to Edmund Cox's inner workings, but to delve into this place that was so special to him, like a love-struck schoolgirl wanting to know everything about her new boyfriend. These strange new feelings made her chew the insides of her cheeks. She tried not to acknowledge them, even though the disturbing progression of them left her uneasy, even a little afraid.

Getting up off the floor, Lori went to her backpack, tucking away the items she'd taken out the night before. She looked to Abby. Her back was turned to Lori, so she couldn't tell if she was awake or not. She'd been wiped out last night and refused to get up even for a hot meal. Even when Jo-Jo got to licking the top of her head, Abby hadn't stirred. Lori shuffled toward the kitchen area, dull aches making themselves known. As a waitress, she worked on her feet all day, but a full day of hiking was still more exercise than she was used to, and Buzz's bed was firmer than her own. She arched her back in a stretch and took a long drink from her water bottle, nearly dropping it when she heard the scream.

In his chair, Buzz cried out with horror, as if he were being immolated by fire rather than sitting back in his chair. Jo-Jo immediately went to him and started licking his face to wake him from his nightmare. Buzz's eyes snapped open, bloodshot, jittering. His dental plate shifted in his mouth, his words rushing out in a garbled mess.

"River run red. Go shout hollerin', now. Oh, my Hattie."

Abby stirred and sat up. Lori placed her hand on Buzz's shoulder. "You all right, Buzz?"

The old man blinked his dream away. "Hot damn. One helluva bad dream. Black cat musta crossed my trail. Ain't had no nightmare like that since . . . well . . . long time."

There always seemed to be things on the tip of Buzz's tongue, things Lori wished she could pull out of him. Something told her they were keys of a different sort, the kind that could unlock the mystery she pursued. But there simply wasn't time to sit around Buzz's country shack talking about his past. There was something there, a darkness beneath the surface, but expunging it would be pulling a sword from stone. Seeing Abby rise from her slumber, Lori straightened up.

"Well," she said, "we really appreciate your hospitality, Buzz. You've been a great host. But we best be traveling on now."

Buzz sat up with a groan and rose to his feet by bracing himself on Jo-Jo's back. Bones popped in the old man's knees and ankles.

"Y'all ain't gonna get nowheres, ya know."

"Huh?"

Buzz pointed to Abby as she slid into her crutches. "Long as your sista be walkin' in them sticks, y'all ain't gonna get too far. Trail gives out up a ways yonder. Nothin' but black rock on the shore and uphill mountain walkin' after that. Gonna be too hard for her, sure nuff."

Lori's shoulders fell with a sigh. Buzz was right. The trek would be impossible for Abby once the trail ended, and it had to end sometime.

"Is there a chance we'll reach The River Man before the path gets too rough?"

Buzz shook his head. "Ya still don't get it do ya? That River Man be hocus pocus. Ya'll chasin' somebody either a legend or already six feet in the ground. Best thing ya can do is head on home now."

"I can't do that."

"Girl, ya need to listen to what I done told ya."

GONE TO SEE THE RIVER MAN

"There has to be another way to get upriver." Buzz looked away, and then Lori knew. "A boat. You said you have a boat to go fishing in, right? Tell me you have a boat."

Buzz shook his head again, eyes on the floor. "Ain't takin' ya up that river. This be where Buzz's hospitality ends."

"Please, this is the only way we can get there."

His eyes were no longer bloodshot. They were clear as a crystal lake and lucid, but there was a hardness behind them, something stern but fatherly.

"Bad nuff ya takin' your poor sista who don't know no betta. Ain't gonna rope ol' Buzz Fledderjohn into no ghost chase. Believe that."

Lori ran a hand through her hair, resisting the compulsion to bite her nails, which were already gnawed down to jagged nubs. She was getting as bad as Abby.

"I'll pay you," she said. "I ain't got much money, but I can give you what I have saved up. Almost five hundred bucks. That buys a lot of Wild Irish Rose and Mail Pouch. Not to mention kibble for Jo-Jo. And, no offense but, looking around this place, it doesn't seem like you have much for money."

Buzz glanced at her, giving her a glimmer of hope, but then he shook his head again, rubbing his chin. Lori spoke before he could say no again.

"I'm not asking you to be on the water for days and days. Just take us upriver today, okay? Based on what my friend told me, we shouldn't have trouble finding it. He said the shack's right off the river. I mean, we're bound to see it."

Buzz's eyes stayed on the floor even as Abby approached.

"I wanna go sailing, Sissy. Mr. Buzz is gonna take us sailing?"

Lori didn't answer. Instead she waited for the old man to.

"Alright," he said. "One trip up Hollow River 'n' back. That's it and that's all."

Lori beamed. Abby clapped her hands, making Lori feel like they were children again and Dad had announced they were going to the drive-in on an autumn night. Beside them, Jo-Jo groaned in disapproval, but she paid the mutt no mind.

"*Sailing, sailing,*" Abby sang, "*sailing with Sissy all day.*"

•••

The rain had dissipated but the sulking clouds remained, putting the daylight on mute. Down the trail, Lori had to support Abby's descent until they reached the riverbank. The waters were calmer this morning. The river lapped at the rocks with wet kisses, its hefty body flowing through the valley like green magma.

Buzz's boat was just big enough for the three of them. It had a small motor, but Buzz also kept paddles inside, explaining that the motor was an ornery thing and only worked when it wanted to. Lori was just grateful to have any boat at all. It was the only thing that could salvage this weird quest. Last night she'd had trouble drifting off, sure this mission was crumbling apart no matter how hard she gripped it. Now her nerves had settled to a manageable quiver, the pain of self-doubt subsiding for the time being. It was a fanged snake that always returned, but for the moment it was coiled in a far corner of her consciousness, subdued. The only thing that worried her now was the lack of life jackets, but she figured she'd been blessed with enough as it was. It was never wise to ask for more than the bare essentials. Lori had learned that over the years. A woman rarely gets what she needs, let alone what she wants.

Buzz helped Abby into the boat and she giggled as it wobbled beneath her, not having the good sense to worry about falling over. Concerns for Abby's safety were left solely to her sister. Lori joined them, sitting at the bow, Buzz at the stern, Abby in the middle, which Lori considered the safest place, provided she didn't have to do any rowing.

The motor started and the boat inched forward, parting the waters like vapor, and as they entered the river the sound of woodland creatures echoed off the mountains in a lonesome song. Lori looked back at the guitar resting by Buzz's side. When she'd asked why he was bringing it, he'd said he didn't want to get bored out on the water while looking for a boogeyman. She supposed there would be times they would just have to drift so they could really scan the tree line for shacks along the shore. Still, it seemed an odd choice for him to take a guitar over a fishing pole, but musicians were like that. Matt had brought his stupid bass guitar with him on every trip they ever took. It had driven Lori nuts. Hopefully Buzz played better than her ex-boyfriend did. It wouldn't be difficult.

The thrum of the motor was lulling, the waters hypnotic. Gazing out into the crevices of the mountain, Lori felt somehow detached from herself, as if she were floating in a black dream. It was colder out on the water and the fuzz on her arms rose, the delicate skin prickling beneath like a plucked chicken. She wasn't sure where this feeling of dread was coming from, but she suddenly felt weightless in a manner that left her entirely too vulnerable, as if she'd been tossed from an airplane. It was the same sensation she got when a rollercoaster descended, only more hollowing. Riding on this river was coring her. The trees bent toward her on both sides, besetting her with their flame-colored leaves and long, black arms, as if wanting to rip her flesh away. Her mouth felt filled with sand, heart fused with electric cocaine.

I'm having a panic attack.

The snake of self-doubt has awoken.

But it was more than that. The dread was unlike anything she'd felt before—a thick, pulsing thing. Its power throbbed at the back of her throat like a forceful lover. A tender predator, but a predator nonetheless.

"We're sailing, Sissy!"

Abby's joy snapped Lori out of her dark reverie and she was grateful to be rescued. She was no longer sure if she'd been conscious. Had the whirring motor and rock of the boat caused her to doze into a quick nightmare? She'd slept poorly on Buzz's cot and, his syrupy coffee undrinkable, she'd had no caffeine to reanimate her.

"*Sailing, sailing! Sailing with Sissy and Mr. Buzzy.*" Abby turned back to Buzz and pointed at her Red Sox cap. "This B goes buzz-buzz, just like you. It's not just a letter. It's a bee. It can fly."

The old man smiled at her then looked up to Lori, giving her a wink. Lori smiled back, but it was an empty smile, void of any meaning. She was pondering the strange feeling that had soaked her a moment ago, so distracted by it she almost missed the river shack on the eastern bank.

"There!" she said, pointing.

It was a shack small enough to make Buzz's and Edmund's look like mansions. At first she'd thought it was an outhouse, but as they approached she saw a glow behind a filthy window and crumbling front steps.

"Ain't the one ya want," Buzz said. "That there's Deacon Jones's place."

"Deacon?"

"Aw, yeah. He's a reveren' but everybody just call him Deacon. Ol' buzzard. Older than even me if you can believe anybody could be. He's screwy in the head, but he ain't no River Man."

A reverend?

"We met someone," she said, "before hitting the trail. A real old man. He wore a black suit with a white shirt, like a preacher. And he sang some sort of gospel song; something about gathering at the river."

Buzz nodded. "Yep. That be him."

"That's his shack? The start of the trail is miles and miles from here. And he was walking. How could he walk that far, especially with the land being so rocky? I mean, he must have been eighty years old."

"Dunno. He's a weird wolf. Y'all see him again, best steer clear. Deacon ain't right."

GONE TO SEE THE RIVER MAN

Lori recalled the unease she'd felt at the mere sight of the man, how she'd tucked Abby into the bushes, bear mace in hand.

"What do you mean?" she asked.

Buzz's face darkened, wrinkles contorting it. "Jones used this river to baptize his followers, back when he had 'em. He believes in some kinda Christian faith that he done pieced together from 'em all. Kinda his own religion—not God's word, but the word of Jones. He thought sufferin' was the only way to connect with Jesus, so when he baptized, he baptized *hard*. He'd put ya under the water long enough for it to hurt. Believe that.

"Deacon had himself two babies. One-a his followers—a lil' girl no older than fourteen—she done give birth to them twins and died doin' so. Deacon had a boy and girl he wanted to baptize for the Lord, so he went on down to the riverbank and held them newborn babies under, one in each hand. He did it too long, and his children done drown, just like that. Ain't been right in the head since. Don't think he was all that right to begin with."

Lori gazed out at the water, hands clenching her knees as she imagined two infant faces screaming beneath the river, mouths filling with water, their father's hands wrapped around their fragile ribs like talons.

"He ought to be in jail," Lori said. "Or an asylum."

"Well, yeah. But you just don't know Killen. Things are different 'round here. This river don't flow like no other, and this land don't have the same rules as where y'all come from. Don't think there's any rules down in this valley at all."

Buzz fell silent, eyes going distant as he watched the water ahead. It opened in curtains that flowed without end, leaving a trail behind them, a fading memory of a journey just begun.

Buzz's fingers moved like scrambling spider legs across the strings of his guitar, his other hand using the metal slide, creating a drunken, dream world sound. His voice was a rich baritone, gravel and velvet.

"Down in the hollow, where the river runs so deep. Down in the hollow, that's where my baby goes to weep."

The strumming of the chords reverberated, adding emphasis to the morose lyrics. Buzz's eyes were closed and his head was tilted back, as if the song was being passed down to him from some higher power.

"So if you hear me howlin', where the whisperin' cedars blow, you'll know I lost my darlin', to the waters down below."

Oblivious to the song's bleakness, Abby swayed to the music, smiling. Lori was less enthusiastic. While Buzz was certainly talented, his song was making her chest feel cold, as if the internal organs had been scooped out. The song suggested grief, suicide, death. She didn't want thoughts like those swirling through her head, not when she was on a mission to prove herself to a man—she was beginning to realize—she cared for more deeply than she'd cared to admit, even to herself. Friendship wasn't as obsessive as this, nor as intense. This river quest was powered by a form of love, however warped it may be. She didn't want to be reminded of all the things love was supposed to help her escape.

But Buzz was helping her. She couldn't have gotten this far without him, so she kept her mouth shut and let the old man sing. When he finished, she was relieved he didn't start on another song. The first two had been upbeat, but this blues ballad had strummed a sensitive chord within her.

They'd been on the river for hours. They'd seen one row of dilapidated, uninhabited shacks on the bank, some of which had been half-swallowed by the river. The rotted wood sulked against the rocks like used toothpicks. Abby's initial giddiness for being on the water began to fade and she grew restless, so Lori gave her a juice box.

"Got me an ass-pocket fulla whiskey," Buzz said, pulling a flask from his slacks. "A lil' nip can help keep us warm."

GONE TO SEE THE RIVER MAN

He took a pull on the flask then held it out to Lori.

"Maybe later," she said.

He shrugged, grinning as he brought it back to his lips. Lori was grateful he had the sense not to offer any to Abby. But Buzz was right. They did need to keep warm. The farther they journeyed, the further the temperature dropped. It was a damp cold that rattled her bones. It seemed to emanate from the river itself, the arctic waters sharing what lay beneath. They were adrift now, giving the engine a rest, but water continued to sprinkle over the bow of the boat and each drop felt like ice.

Lori slumped. She was cold and tired and hungry. She wanted to go home. The excitement of doing something important for Edmund had begun to wane. She still wanted to complete the task, but she wanted it over with already.

"Y'all ready to turn back now?" Buzz asked.

Apparently her exhaustion showed.

"No," Lori said. "Not yet."

But there would never be a *yet*. She would keep going until she got there. This was for her man, her love, her everything. She couldn't allow the only light in her miserable world to fade. She had to overcome that snake of doubt no matter how much venom it spat.

What are you talking about? She shook her head. *You're not in love with Edmund!*

Are you?

Thoughts of him had been changing so gradually that she'd only vaguely noticed. But now they were smacking her in the face, hard. She'd been thinking of him in a warmer light despite seeing up close the horror he was capable of. Was it the added mystery of this journey that drew her more to him? Her need to complete this quest had become all-consuming. She simply could not fail Edmund. She cared about him too much now; so much it had begun to sting whenever she was faced with obstacles along this river. Wanting to please a man, despite how difficult it was for her personally . . . well, if that wasn't love, what was?

Lori wrapped her arms around her body, as if hugging herself would keep the confusion at bay. Buzz took another pull on his flask, then reached back and started the motor up again. The boat heaved forward and Lori had to brace herself on the plank she sat upon. Abby wobbled but kept upright, and the sudden motion made her giggle. But she looked so pale now, wan and broken, her skin like chalk, her body twisted. Lori tried to push Buzz's song lyrics away, but they were stuck in her head. Looking at her sister, she felt the swelling of nausea at the back of her skull, but knew it wasn't the movement of the boat making her queasy. The nausea was a familiar enemy.

"Sissy . . ."

"Yeah, Abby?"

"You're gonna get fucked."

Lori gasped. She looked to her sister, who was still giggling, her hands curled up to her lips. Lori glanced at Buzz and he was looking back at her, his eyebrows raised.

"Don't talk like that, Abby."

Her sister snickered. "Sissy is gonna get fucked hard by her new boyfriend. She's gonna like it."

"Stop it!"

Now Abby started laughing, growing louder. "Sissy likes to get fucked! Sissy likes to get fucked! Sissy likes—"

Lori grabbed her sister's hoodie and shook her. "Why do you keep saying that? You know that's no way to talk. It's especially no way to talk about your sister."

Abby looked up at her. Lori gasped again. Her sister's eyes were different. They were darker, pupils dilated. The paleness of her flesh made them stand out all the more, two black globes lost in a white squall. When she cackled again, her teeth gleamed even in the gray light of day, looking jagged and chipped. Her lips curdled into a cruel smile.

"I can have him, you know," Abby said.

Lori leaned back.

"I can have your boyfriend," Abby said. "I can take him any time I want. Just like I took David."

Lori snatched a short breath as the pain entered her. It was a memory that had never left her, but one she'd thought had been knocked out of Abby's skull for sure. She hadn't spoken of David in decades. Not since her accident. Why would she bring him up now, and why in such a cruel way? Even if she were just making an attempt at black comedy, it wasn't like Abby to tease and provoke. Buzz seemed just as shocked as Lori was. Out of politeness, he gazed off into the distance, as if nothing were happening. Lori was left speechless, but Abby had finished. She giggled into her balled fists, nothing more.

If she remembers David . . . what else does she remember?

FIFTEEN

DEAREST EDMUND,

There are secrets I want to share with you. They are dark secrets, ones I've never told anyone. I have done bad things. I want you to know that, because it will help you see that we're not so different. I understand how someone can do a terrible thing, how something black and evil can grow inside them and just take over. It can start as jealousy, maybe envy. It can start as greed or anger or hatred or despair. Grief can turn to rage and rot you from the inside out. I know these things just as surely as I know I would take what I have done to my grave, telling no one, if it weren't for you . . .

SIXTEEN

THE TEARS ON HER FATHER'S cheeks made Lori go cold. She'd never seen Dad cry. In her eyes, he was unbreakable. A true silent type, her father rarely expressed his emotions. She knew he loved her, Abby and Mom, but it was a love that had to be expressed without saying the word, a love that had to be felt without many hugs or kisses. He wasn't cold to his family, just reserved. For Lori, that stoic nature had translated into strength.

Seeing Dad cry now took a safety net away. It meant the levee that kept back danger had crumbled. It left Lori feeling unbearably vulnerable, and she instantly regretted all the times she'd wished Dad would show more emotion. She wanted him to be stone again, impenetrable, because that was the Daddy she knew. That was normal.

But nothing was normal anymore.

Across the table, Pete stared at his food, not eating. It was pizza—his favorite. But he hadn't touched a slice. He hadn't eaten a morsel of food in weeks. Mom and Dad had been serving up anything they thought he would touch. Pete's face was sunken, eyelids purple. He looked like he was getting just as much sleep as he was nutrition.

"Please, son," Dad said. "Please. Just one slice."

Pete leaned forward, staring down at the food. Grief pinched at the corners of his mouth and for a moment Lori was sure he was going to tell. Her stomach bottomed out. Sweat formed at the small of her back. Pete had been drifting away ever since that first night in his bedroom, when she had felt something warm in her belly, something that had been brewing there since her first period. Feeling her brother growing hard in her hand, she had started getting wet. Pete was lying on the bed with his eyes closed, so Lori slung one leg over him, then the other. By the time he opened his eyes, she had pushed the bottom of her panties away from her vagina and slipped him inside. His eyes and mouth opened wide and a shiver coursed through every inch of him, including his penis. The feeling of him filling her up was electric. Far more satisfying than when she touched herself. And it wasn't just the sexual pleasure, but the feeling of wholeness and connectivity. She was finally with a boy—finally not a virgin. It was an incredible moment. But it didn't last very long. Pete's second shiver came as he climaxed inside her.

After the thrill was over, and they were left with the wet, sloppy evidence of what they'd done, Lori moved aside just enough for Pete's spent penis to pop out of her. Even in the darkness, she could see his face in the light of the moon, and the look of ecstasy that had been there moments ago had curdled into something sick, something diseased. Her brother looked on the verge of tears—not of sorrow, but of horror. His grimace drove those same feelings deep into Lori, just as deep as his seed had entered her. Only the horror wouldn't dribble out like so much semen. Her heartbeat grew sluggish, fingertips like ice. Something tingled beneath her breast, then twisted into a knot. It was not a horror that came from the act, but rather a horror passed on to her by her brother. The fear and self-loathing she sensed in him was now trying to poison her too. She had to do something.

Still straddling Pete, Lori bent over and whispered in his ear, shushing him.

GONE TO SEE THE RIVER MAN

"It's okay, Pete. It's all okay."

But it wasn't. It never would be again.

That was the first time, but not the last. It had all started with playful experimentation, curiosity. They played doctor in a sense, even though they were both old enough to know better. Then came the dry humping, and then finally, the surprise intercourse. Once she'd had a taste, Lori's hunger for sex grew insatiable. Not only did she want to get good at it, she also craved the shudders that rolled through her body when she was on top of her brother. Pete was always hesitant, but she always managed to coerce him by taking his hand and running it over her breasts or putting his fingers in her mouth. They'd been having sex regularly for almost a month, and while Pete never refused, he never seemed happy about it. He didn't get from their nights together the same thing Lori did. It was as if his body was engaging in something beyond his control. It irritated her. Why did he seem to love it and hate it at the same time? She would have to work harder in her practice rounds with him, to make sure this didn't happen with the boys who would actually count. Practice made perfect, so she kept going back to Pete's room at night, assuring herself that if he didn't fight her he must be okay with it no matter how regretful he seemed in the aftermath. Lori was regretful sometimes too. She knew what they were doing was taboo, but who was it hurting? They needed to learn about sex somehow. Better for it to be with someone they knew and trusted.

But then Pete had stopped eating. He lost interest in playing baseball and ignored his Super Nintendo. He stayed in bed as much as their parents allowed. Pete was crumbling inward, and Lori was watching him fall with a detached awareness. She'd always wanted to believe she could ignore a problem into no longer existing. But this problem had been germinating within Pete from the moment she'd put him inside of her, and now the black ooze of it was exuding and showing itself for the whole world to see.

One night, he finally tried to stop her. She tiptoed into his room like usual, wearing a cotton nightgown with no panties on underneath. She couldn't see him, but from the sound of his voice she knew he was standing close to the doorway. He'd been waiting for her.

"Don't," he said.

Lori stepped forward, reaching blindly. She found his arm. He recoiled.

"It's okay, Pete. Everything's okay."

He sniffled. "No. It's not okay. Stop saying it's okay when you know it's not."

Lori shifted her weight to the other foot, uncomfortable in her skin. "Pete, it's fine. Nothing bad is gonna happen. Don't worry."

Her eyes had begun to adjust to the darkness, and she could see his silhouette before her now, so small and thin, as fragile as a porcelain doll.

"Please . . ." he muttered.

She shushed him just like she had the first time, a soft, calming hush. Now when she touched him, he stepped into her, exciting her down below, but then he pushed his head into her shoulder, flung his arms around her neck, and started to cry. At first he was merely blubbering, but through the snot and sobs he began to make sense.

Lori went hollow. It was as if a wind had moved through her. Pete's words cut her innards, filling her with heat. She wanted to scream and vomit.

"No," was all Lori could say.

"But we *have* to. We have to *stop*."

"No."

"Lori . . . we can't keep on doing this." Pete was bawling now. "I'm . . . I dunno . . . *scared*."

"Stop it, Pete. Just stop it." She was whispering but her words came out fast and sharp. "Stop talking like this."

"It's wrong . . . Lori, it's wrong . . ."

"You don't seem to think it's wrong when we're *doing* it."

Pete turned away in self-disgust. "But—"

"But nothing. You've gotten your needs taken care of, but what about mine? I need this."

She didn't explain why. Admitting she lacked the skills to get boys was not something she was going to do with her brother or anyone else.

"No more," Pete said. "I'm not doing it no more. I don't . . . I don't even want to *think* about it anymore, Lori."

The sourness in Lori's stomach rose and boiled. Pete was so damned selfish. He'd gotten what he wanted, blowing his wad again and again, and now he was trying to bail out of the exchange before he'd served his purpose. She had to resist the urge to punch him.

"Get on the bed," she ordered.

"What? No. I told you—"

"Fine" she snapped. "Then I'll tell Mom and Dad."

Pete froze.

"That's right," Lori said, forced tears burning in the corners of her eyes as she bluffed. "If you don't give me what I need, I'll tell Mom and Dad what we've been doing. And I'll tell them you forced me."

In the moonlight, Pete was a ghost of a boy. His shocked expression made him look even younger, and the innocence Lori saw in him disgusted her. It was a lie. Pete was not a sweet, little kid anymore. He was a selfish pecker. It was time he was reminded she was older than he was. She was in charge.

"Lori . . ."

"Don't talk. Just get on the bed, or I swear I'll tattle."

"Please . . . don't . . ."

"You know how much it'll break Mom's heart? Do you know how pissed off Dad is gonna be? Things will never, *ever* be the same if I tell on you. They probably won't want you to be their son anymore. They'll send you away somewhere—a youth ranch or some other awful place. You'll never see Mom and Dad and Abby again.

You'll never see your friends. I'll tell all of them, Pete. Everyone at school will know what you did and—"

"Stop."

He said it calmly, but she could hear the tears choking him. He moved out of the light and into the shadows at the back of the room. She heard the bed creak and the soft, feathery sound of his pajamas hitting the floor.

In the weeks that followed, her brother began to deteriorate. Now he was wan and empty at the table. It was as if he'd aged, faded to gray. Mom and Dad were struggling not to break down. Lori was the only one who'd touched the pizza. Her parents were too focused on Pete, and Abby, for some reason, was glowering at Lori again. She'd been giving her a lot of strange looks lately. She seemed angry at times, even disgusted.

Lori had an inkling as to why.

Abby must have found out how Lori felt about David, how she loved him more deeply than Abby ever could. Had her sister read her diary? It would be just like her to sneak around behind her back like that. She'd already stolen David; maybe she was stealing from Lori's room too.

When Abby gave Lori the evil eye, she wanted to shoot one right back but couldn't hold her gaze for long. Abby was the oldest. She had the more dominating personality. Of the three siblings, she'd always been the boss, the third in command under their parents. As much as Lori wanted to overthrow Abby, or at least break free of her rule, she simply couldn't rise up against her. So when Abby stared at her like that, Lori's eyes fell and her shoulders caved in. Her cheeks turned pink and her skin crept. Silent treatment had fallen between the two sisters and Lori didn't dare break it for fear it would set something off in Abby, something never seen but always lying dormant, ready as the horns of hell.

"Pete," Mom said. "This can't go on like this."

Pete's chin dimpled, lips trembling as if he were about to say something. Lori's shoulders went tight. It would be so easy for her brother to unleash a great ruin upon them. How much could a boy take before he cracked? It was only a matter of time, wasn't it?

No.

She couldn't think that way. Pete wouldn't tell. After all, he'd been terrified by Lori's threat to do so. The secret was devouring him, but he would never release it. It hung around his neck like an anchor on a chain.

"I think we should see a counselor," Mom said, addressing the family as a whole. "We have to band together at a time like this."

•••

The rope that held the swing had turned green during the rainy fall and by November it was withering away, string by string. It seemed like every part of Lori's childhood was withering, every trace rapidly being erased. At first she welcomed the transition. She'd been sexually awoken, and that put her on the path to becoming a woman. But now that her family was shattering, Lori found herself wishing she could return to a simpler time when Dad was strong, Mom was happy, and Abby didn't hate her.

She even found herself wondering if what she had done to Pete really was wrong. At first she'd told herself he was just being a baby, that he couldn't handle not getting his way. As his anorexia worsened, she tried to convince herself he was only doing it to break her, to force her to stop forcing him. He probably thought he could intimidate her with his self-harm. She told herself it was an empty threat, nothing more. Eventually he would get so hungry he would have to give in. Without food he would die. He wouldn't take things that far . . .

She pushed herself forward on the balls of her feet, swinging, hearing the rope strain, careful not to swing out over the ledge. It was okay to plan a lunge into the swimming hole, but a sudden tumble could cause her to hit the rocks that jutted out from the hillside and ran along the shoreline below. Lori stared down at their slick, black surfaces, all gleaming like polished marble as the water flowed around them. The frothing chaos of that darkness was like a reflection of her rambling mind. Her thoughts were of misery and despair, a load too heavy for a teenage girl. She wanted to cry, to release a scream that would echo through the valley, singing her own pain back at her.

The clouds had gone from gray to black, churning with the threat of rain. The air smelled clean as ice. She knew she should go back home before she got soused, but wanted to stay by the creek's edge. This place held so many happy memories. It had always made her feel good to come to this spot. That is, until she'd seen Abby here with David on top of her. In the months since she'd caught them, she'd continued to come out here and search for the joy the clearing once held, seeking and never finding. Abby screwing David had buried it alive, this once special place tainted by their dripping, groaning love. She figured she should find someplace new, but for some reason was unable to give it up. Doing so would mean that joy truly was dead and gone.

Sliding off the swing, Lori dusted off her jeans. Dead leaves crackled beneath her boots as she walked along the edge of the cliff, still staring at the rushing water. The stream was alive today, swollen with rain. The creek that broke off from it was wider than ever and the circular channel where they swam swirled like a dust devil. She imagined sailing off upon the waters, leaving the sorrow of her present day behind her like so much ash. One day she would have her own car to drive her away, her own apartment to start a new life in. But she had three years until she turned eighteen. The number was a brutal eternity.

There was a rustle in the thicket and Lori jolted and looked up. Someone was coming through a cluster of dead bushes, heading toward her. She thought of bears and bucks, bobcats and coyotes. It wasn't until she saw her sister's face that she was able to breathe again. Abby was dressed heavier than Lori was. She had her long winter coat pulled close, hands in the pockets, cheeks rosy from the cold. Lori wondered if she looked the same way. Somehow she hadn't felt the bitter temperature, not even on the edge of the cliff where the breeze never stopped.

Abby stepped into the clearing. Her eyes were like glaciers—wet and blue like their mother's, blue as a sky in June. There was no trace of happiness in them. They'd gone nearly as dark as Pete's, hardened by all that had happened. They seemed pushed farther away, dulled by something buried deep within.

Abby stopped a few feet from Lori and the clouds groaned with thunder as the storm crept in. Abby pulled her coat even tighter, a security blanket. This time when Lori met her gaze, it was Abby who couldn't lock eyes for long. She bit her bottom lip and hung her head.

Lori's voice was just above a whisper. "Abby?"

Her sister looked like a shadow of herself. Something important had detached, something as vital as a heartbeat.

"Abby?"

"Don't."

Lori paused. "Don't what?"

But Abby didn't answer. Her hair blew about from beneath her beanie and she didn't tuck it away when it fluttered before her face.

"I know," Abby said.

Lori swallowed hard.

Oh no. She saw me. She saw me when she was having sex with David.

"I . . ." But Lori couldn't find the words to defend herself with. "I, um . . ."

"What is wrong with you?"

Lori crossed her arms. "Hey—"

"How could you do something like this? It's not his fault. You're the one who should know better."

Heat rose up Lori's neck. *Know better?* So that's what her sister thought of her? That she should have known David would never want anything to do with a pathetic little virgin like her? And it *wasn't* his fault that he liked Abby better? Why? Because Abby was the pretty one, the charmer, the dream date every boy in school thought about when love songs came on the radio? Abby was saying Lori wasn't worthy of getting a good guy, let alone David. She was saying she didn't have the same value as Abby did.

"Fuck you, Abby! You don't know anything!"

Her sister blinked with disbelief. Lori had surprised both of them. She rarely cursed and had never stood up to her sister like this. She'd thought she never would. It seemed Abby had that same preconceived notion.

"I do know," Abby said. "I know it all, Lori. I saw you—"

"*You know it all.* Yeah, that's you all over, isn't it, Abby? You're a stupid know-it-all. You're just the best at everything, aren't you? I guess that's why you always get your way. That's why you got David instead of me, right? 'Cause you're so goddamn perfect!"

Abby blinked. "David? What are you talking about?"

"I loved him! You knew I did, but you took him anyway." Lori struggled to speak against the lump rising in her throat. "You could have any boy you want, and you had to take the one boy I was crazy about."

"Oh my God. That's not what this is about."

"It's about you being better than me. Well, I can be good at things too, you know. David cares about me too. Maybe not enough to climb on top of me right here in the woods like a couple of animals but—"

"Lori, stop."

"Do you like getting fucked in the dirt? Like a dog?"

Abby stepped forward so quickly Lori didn't have time to do anything but flinch. She took Lori's flannel in her fists and pulled her in.

"And what about you, Lori? Do you like fucking *your own brother?*"

GONE TO SEE THE RIVER MAN

The earth beneath Lori's feet turned to quicksand.

Her body shook as if electrocuted, sickness nestling in, panic rising in heat waves.

"Wha-what?"

"You saw me and David, huh? Well I saw you . . . you and Pete." Abby's words came out like she was gagging. "You're disgusting. He's just a boy . . . your brother! *Your little brother!*"

Lori swayed, feeling faint. She welcomed the possibility of unconsciousness, of escape of any kind. If she fell asleep, maybe she'd awake to find this was all just a terrible dream. Abby *couldn't* know about her and Pete. It shattered everything. Her world had already been drained of all color, now it was in danger of splintering into shards of its former self, making it impossible to mend together again. If her sister knew . . . then . . .

"You need to tell them," Abby said.

Now Lori did feel the cold. "N-n-no."

"The counselor can't help Pete if he doesn't know the root of his problem. He's sick, Lori—sick because of what you did. You have to tell Mom and—"

"No!"

"—Dad. Look, we can do it together. I'll be there to help you do it."

Lori put her hands to her face. "No! No! No!"

"Lori, you have to."

She pulled away from Abby and went to the swing, clutching the rope in both hands, resting her forehead against it and watching the stream carry away dead leaves, dead lives, dead dreams. The wind had grown blustery, causing the water to explode against the rocks.

She felt Abby's presence behind her.

When her sister took her shoulder, the burning within Lori ignited, her fear and anger volcanic. She spun around, screeching and cursing as she lashed out. Abby tried to wrap her arms around Lori to keep her from flailing, but she raged against her, knocking her away.

Abby stumbled backward, toward the edge of the cliff.

Lori glimpsed something in her sister's eyes she'd not seen since they were children. Since becoming a happy, pretty teenager with the world at her feet, Abby hadn't had to worry about anything. But now, as she struggled near the edge, her eyes came alive, the whites of them glaring. Her mouth fell open as she rolled her arms in the air in an attempt to regain her balance.

A sudden calm came over Lori. Seeing terror crawl across her big sister's face had abated her frenzy. There was such fear there. Lori loved to witness it. It meant Abby wasn't unbreakable after all. The beauty and popularity could not help her here. Her good luck had just run out, and it was about damn time.

Abby tried to speak but could find no voice, and though her wobbling lasted only seconds, to Lori the moment seemed to linger on, time stopping so she could savor every second. She'd waited so long to see her sister fail. This made things even. And when Abby couldn't right herself, she reached out for Lori in one last effort to escape her fate.

Lori lifted one hand, but only to wave goodbye.

SEVENTEEN

THE RIVER WAS CHANGING.
 The water had gone from green to a muddied purple. Now it was morphing into an unnatural burgundy. When Lori glanced over the edge of the boat, the murk drifted sluggishly, more oil than water. Pebbles and twigs scattered through the sludge like the death of a galaxy. She looked back at Buzz. He was taking another sip from his flask. He'd been hitting it a lot these past few hours and she could hardly blame him. The trip had been uneventful and now they were moving slower, cautious of the rock clusters. Here the river grew narrower, the trees on either side closing in, cloaking everything in a pall of darkness. The day had gone wintry mean and a thin mist hovered in the air, stacking the miseries.

Abby had curled into a ball and was resting her head against Lori's thigh. Her eyes were closed but Lori wasn't sure if she was asleep. Buzz wasn't totally drunk, but he was slurring his words a little.

"River gets all worse up ahead now. Ain't just rocks, but rapids. This ol' boat can't handle them no ways."

Lori nodded but said nothing. They had to press on, but she could see what Buzz was saying. There were more rocks here, and more dips up ahead. And the water was still changing.

"How come it looks like that?" she asked.

"What's that now?"

"The water. It looks red."

"Red?"

"Yeah, dark red." She pointed where the current surged, a crimson syrup. "Can't you see it?"

Buzz squinted. "Shit. My peepers ain't as good as they useta been. Lil' bit colorblind, ya know."

There was a rustle in the woods to their left, and when Lori turned to look a damp cold settled in. The temperature dropped upon her like an invisible fog, causing her to shudder. Leaning in the direction of the sound, she saw something pale and lithe twist through the black thicket. The bramble splintered and popped as the thing darted behind their cover. Lori thought it must be a wild animal, until she spotted pale, human feet scampering through the brush.

"Hello?" she called out.

The feet vanished in a rustle of dead leaves. Whoever it was, they were running.

"Hey! Hello?"

"Whatchoo doin'?" Buzz asked. "Ain't nobody out there."

"I saw someone. I saw their feet."

Buzz sighed. "Ya ain't seen nothin' or nobody. You's just tryin' to find a reason to stay out here when I went on told ya we can't keep sailin' up this river no mo—"

A light, fluttery laughter rose out of the woods like music—the laughter of a little boy. Lori's whole body tensed. Behind her, Buzz had fallen silent.

Abby stirred. "Petey?"

Lori's chest curled inward. Though she'd never gotten seasick before, she now felt a terrible nausea oozing through her. She shifted out from under Abby's weight, struggling to get her hands on the edge of the boat to pull her head over. She held her eyes tight against the heave but, realizing there was no fighting it, she opened her eyes again and gazed into the river below, a river the color of blood.

Lori caught her reflection. Her face was a red death mask, contorting with sickness, aged by this foul sense of dread. She felt as if she were going to vomit her full innards, eviscerating herself with one brutal regurgitation. But when she finally began to heave it was dry, and in a way that was worse. Her body convulsed, veins showing themselves, but she produced nothing.

The childish laughter bounced off the mountains like bird songs, sounding unbearably innocent. Lori shut her eyes, as if that could help her not hear her brother's lost joy. Exhausted, she draped her body on the edge of the boat and a small wave splashed her arm hanging over the side.

The water was warm.

She drew back her hand to see the blood running down her forearm as if she'd slit her wrist. Buzz leaned toward her, staring.

"I see colors better up close."

He reached down and ran one hand through the water. When he pulled it up, the color was as sharp as red ink.

"You smell that?" Lori asked. "It's like . . . copper."

Buzz nodded. "I think it's time we get on back."

"Buzz . . ."

The old man's face had gone tombstone gray. His eyes darted back and forth, as if something were creeping up on him.

Abby's eyes fluttered open. "Sissy . . ."

"We can't turn back now, Buzz. Please, we have to—"

"Looka here," he said, holding out his dripping hand. "That smell ain't copper. It be blood."

Lori couldn't deny what it looked like, but she couldn't believe it either.

"Maybe we hit something."

Buzz shook his head and took up a paddle. "That ain't somethin' *in* the river. That *is* the river!"

"Maybe that little boy put something in the water."

But Buzz wasn't listening. He was muttering silent prayers as he spun the boat around. "Oh, Hattie. Watch over me, darlin'. I never done believed it."

"Believed what?"

"A river of flesh," he said, his eyes wide. "They say The River Man lives up where the river turns to flesh. But I been up this way before! Water ain't never looked like this here!"

He wiped his arm on his slacks, staining them.

"You're bleeding," Abby said.

Buzz stared at Abby as if he were surprised she could talk. "Ain't my blood, honey."

"But you're going to bleed."

Buzz looked away. "You best not say things like that. Not now."

"Old men bleed so easy."

He took to paddling, moving faster than Lori would have thought his aged bones were capable of. She reached over Abby and grabbed at the oar, but Buzz wouldn't stop.

"The river can't really be blood," she said. "It must be coral or mud or something."

"River of flesh . . . they done told me . . ."

"Well if that's what they said, maybe it was just a dramatic way of saying the river runs red near where he lives. That would mean we're close. The River Man must be here, right?"

Buzz shook his head as if trying to knock something out of it.

"We've come this far," Lori said. "We can't turn back now."

"Ain't goin' no further."

He kept paddling.

She reached for the oar with both hands. "Stop."

Buzz shook her loose. "Damn it, woman! Can't you see we're messin' with somethin' we shouldn't?"

Lori grabbed at the oar again, putting her shoulder into Buzz's chest. Nearly drunk, he lost his balance and dropped the oar. The boat wobbled, sending bloody waves over the sides.

Abby giggled. "The boat is bleeding, Sissy."

Lori slid on the slick, red liquid.

It is *blood.*

She peered upriver. A winding current of gore sluiced through the stone crevices and rolled beneath fallen branches, carrying dead leaves the color of fire. They tumbled past the boat and fluttered through the air like burning embers, and when Lori watched them go skyward there was a quick flash of pink lightning behind the curtain of storm clouds. Abby laughed and clapped her hands. Lori turned to her, a chill shooting through her insides. Abby's eyes were so dark, the whites suppressed to mere specs. Her lip was curled, hair matted to her head. She looked diseased, deranged, possessed.

"Gone to see The River Man," she said. "The River Man gonna *see us.*"

Buzz shot back up. "We gotta get the hell outta here!"

But they were too close now. Lori could feel it. It was in the sudden spread of cold air and the body temperature of the water. She could smell it on top of the surging gore below. There was an energy here, grim and vicious, the same intense aura that encircled the man she now knew she desired. Edmund Cox billowed through space and time in a black sphere of energy. When you were in the man's presence, the gravity of all he had done pulled at you with the intensity of a gas giant planet. And here, on this river of flesh, she could feel that same darkness, rich and organic, pulsating like a newborn heart.

She was so close now. So very close.

When Buzz reached for the oar again, Lori hit him.

"We're not going back!"

The boat shook as Lori went at the old man, and Abby scooted behind them, watching with huge, possum eyes. Lori punched Buzz in the mouth, and he shoved her so hard she nearly fell over the edge, barely grasping her seat in time. The old man snatched the oar, baring his teeth, his face ugly with anger. He got up on his knees and raised the oar high, a batter to the plate.

"I don't wanna do this, but—"

Lightning cracked the sky, and when the flash was over the world was stained red, the sky becoming a reflection of the river. There were only two shades to everything now—crimson and shadow. Buzz gazed up. Lori froze too, hypnotized. The woods reminded her of the dark room she'd once developed film in before she'd given up on photography. The red was deep and uncompromising, letting no other colors sneak past it. The storm writhed, otherworldly.

But Buzz still had the oar.

"Hell," he muttered.

He grimaced at Lori and she reached for her bag, trying to remember which pocket she'd put the bear mace in. From the flash in his eyes, he must have known she was going for a weapon. The oar came up.

"Woman, don't make me—"

There was a snapping sound, much like an egg hitting the floor—*crack!*

Buzz went still. His eyes rolled and his jaw fell slack. A trickle of blood poured from the top of his head and ran down the bridge of his nose, followed by a steady stream.

"Oh, Hattie . . ."

He dropped into Lori, and without him to block her view she could see Abby crouched behind the old man, a blood-speckled crutch in her hands.

As Buzz went slack, the oar splashed into the river. Lori cried out.

"No!"

Buzz was too heavy for her to push off in time to grab for the oar. It floated away on the rushing water like so much autumn leaves, gone forever. Lori shifted out from beneath Buzz's dead weight. She could only hope he was still alive and the boat's motor would be enough to get them where they needed to go and back. She put her hands to his head and lifted it up.

"Buzz?"

He was entirely limp. His eyes were halfway closed and the lids didn't flutter when she shook him. With his head tilted toward her, she could see just how badly Abby had hurt him. His skull was split down the center, the tissue stripped away in segments, revealing indented bone. She could hardly believe her weak, crippled sister could have produced such a devastating blow.

"I told him," Abby said.

"What?"

"I told him he was gonna bleed."

Lori swallowed hard. "Abby? What's gotten into you?"

But Lori already knew. It was these woods, this river. It was the very nature of their quest. Lori had felt the sinister energy here, and Abby must have sensed it too, but she was reacting to it in her own way. Her mind did not operate normally. It went off path and sometimes got lost for a long time.

"Is he dead?" Abby asked with a dull curiosity, showing no concern.

Lori held her fingertips to Buzz's throat, finding no pulse. She took his wrist, knowing the result would be the same. Her hands trembled as she withdrew.

"Oh, Abby . . ."

But there was nothing else to say.

Abby stopped the old guy. She saved Sissy. It didn't make her feel good though. She didn't feel much of anything now. She was beset by numbness and dullness, boredom. Not like earlier today, when she'd felt afraid that Sissy would leave her, or when she'd been furious with Sissy without knowing why. She'd had to say bad things then, naughty things. Even the F word. She thought it was kinda funny, but a mean sort of funny, an *angry* funny.

But that's what Sissy wanted. To F-U-C-K her new boyfriend. Abby remembered fucking too. There was a boy inside her once. She could even remember his name now. *David.* A boy from long ago, before the change. But it was all very nice, what she remembered. She didn't know why he was gone, but suspected he must have made Sissy mad. Abby didn't know why. She just knew it was so. Abby also knew now that she was once much better than Sissy. The river had just reminded her.

It was reminding her of a lot of things.

•••

The motor was easy enough to figure out. Though it was stubborn, Lori got it going and steered the boat toward a soft slope by the river's edge, shutting it off as they drew closer to the bank. The boat drifted through the red hell Killen had become, sailing slow as a ghost ship.

She was still struggling to wrap her mind around what was happening. It was easier to focus on the murder her sister had committed than it was to figure out what was going on in these woods. Strangely, the murder kept her centered in reality.

They had to get rid of the body. She supposed the best thing to do was bury Buzz, but that would mean they'd have to haul his carcass into the woods. This would be a treacherous, uphill struggle. The land was too mean for it. But she couldn't stand the idea of sailing him somewhere else. She didn't want the body in the boat with them for one second longer.

And she wasn't sure how she felt about Abby's stoic behavior. In a way, it was a relief she wasn't hysterical because it made things easier to manage, but at least if she were freaking out she would seem somewhat normal, or at least what was normal for Abby. The only familiar thing she was doing was petting her rabbit's foot. At least her eyes looked human again. They were still dark, but not in the freakish way they had been when the river had first turned to blood. Lori tried to tell herself it was just a trick of the light, an illusion caused by the sudden redness, but even the redness itself seemed like a hallucination. It was getting harder to trust her own eyes.

A riverbank of black dirt lay ahead, just large enough to dock the boat upon, but Lori didn't want to get too close. All it would take was one hidden rock to rip the boat's belly out from under them, and then they'd be stranded in these woods, lost in the nightmare they provided. If they could just get the boat to shallow water she wouldn't have to worry about the current taking them if the boat tipped while they were tossing Buzz overboard. They trailed along the bank, and when the land curved the waters calmed. The boat drifted in a comfortable spin.

Lori looked to her sister. "You're gonna have to help me."

"I tried."

"What do you mean?"

"I tried to help, Sissy. But you didn't want my help."

Lori sighed. Her nerves were too tangled to tolerate Abby's nonsense.

"Abby, just help me lift Buzz over the—"

"We could have gone to Mom and Dad together. That's what I wanted to do, remember?"

A sick quiver went through Lori. "Abby . . ."

"You wanna push Buzz into the water."

Lori couldn't reply. When she opened her mouth, there were only clicks and gags.

"Sissy likes to push people in the water. She makes the water run red."

Tears welled in Lori's eyes; Abby's face remained blank. She wasn't expressing these words, merely speaking them, like someone reading off an address or phone number.

How much does she remember?

Even if Abby couldn't put enough pieces together to complete the memory, there was some inkling there, some small window her mind had opened, giving an obstructed view of yesterday. After her fall, she'd stayed in a coma for several days, and once she awoke she could barely tell them who she was. She had no recollection of the accident, so Lori had made one up about the swing breaking while Abby was on it. She even took the time to climb the tree and rip down the moldy rope—no easy task—and toss the swing down onto the rocks where her sister's mangled body lay, her blood turning the swimming hole the color of an opening rose. No one had ever doubted her story, and Abby had never remembered the truth.

These were horrors Lori had never been able to bury deep enough inside herself to keep from resurfacing, but she'd felt confident they were her memories alone. With Pete dead and Abby mentally challenged as a result of her injury, no one knew all the terrible things she had done. They were her private hells to be shared only in intimate discussion with the man she'd grown to love, and only to show him he wasn't evil, that he had merely acted upon sinister urges, just as she had. Lori hadn't been leading him on after all. She had desired him in her subconscious mind, mentally disguising her growing love as a mere act to gain Edmund's trust. But their new kinship was as real as their old cruelties.

All the world is guilty. It's just a matter of degree.

"Abby . . . we have to get him off the boat."

Her sister nodded. "He don't need to see The River Man. Not no more."

Lori reached under the corpse, shifting Buzz to the edge. Abby took his feet.

"Which one's lucky, Sissy?"

"What?"

"The feet. Which is the lucky one?"

Lori grunted, shifting the dead man's weight. Abby placed one of Buzz's legs on the bow, undoing the laces of his boot. It was worn and slipped right off the corpse's foot.

"This one," Abby said. "That's lucky, just like my rabbit's."

"Push!"

"Can I take it?"

"Take what?"

"I want to take his foot with us. For luck."

Lori closed her eyes tight and pushed, unable to give her sister an answer. Pressure thundered through her mind. She lifted with her back turned, pushing with her thighs, and the boat threatened to turn over. Lori screamed in frustration. When she opened her eyes again, Abby was looking at her with her head tilted like a listening dog.

"Oh, alright," Abby said.

She pushed the foot away, slinging the leg over the edge, and then lifted the other one. Together they sent the body overboard. Buzz splashed in a burst of red, the body bobbing in this still pocket of the river before floating backward toward the pull of the current. Lori wondered if they should have weighed him down with rocks so he would sink to the bottom. It was too late now; too late for a lot of things. Watching him drift into the long throat of the river, a fresh fear coiled around Lori.

Did I fail?

The feeling was sudden but absolute. *Failure*—that old, familiar bully.

The only man who understood her was a killer. She'd come out here to prove herself to him. Now she was watching a dead body float away, but she hadn't been the one to commit the murder. Abby had done that.

Abby.

It was always Abby. Even now that she was an imbecile, she was still better than Lori. Abby had killed Buzz, not in an attempt to save Lori but to take something away from her. Murder made Abby more like Edmund than Lori was. They shared something most people never got to experience, and the little bitch had even said she could take Edmund away from her, just as she had taken David. Was she making good on that threat? If Lori had killed Buzz, she would have solidified a deeper connection with the man she loved. She could say she did it just to be closer to him, and if she'd thought of it before it was too late, that would have been true. She'd thought the cruel actions of her past would be enough to prove to Edmund she shared his inner darkness, understood it. She'd allowed her sister to fall off the cliff. She'd taken advantage of her little brother. These acts had destroyed her family. They might be slight compared to ripping innocent people to pieces, as Edmund had done, but these were the darkest corners of Lori's soul. What she'd done in her youth had poisoned her adult life, just as what Edmund had done ruined any chance for him to have a future. She'd believed that gave them a special unity. Now she realized it simply wasn't enough.

What if Niko has already killed for him?

The cunt had the upper hand already, being Asian. Had she taken her devotion to that next level? Lori barely knew the woman, but somehow doubted Niko had murder in her. Still, it was a terrifying possibility.

Then again, Lori didn't think she herself had a murder in her either. She'd never been violent, and while she'd let Abby fall off the cliff, it had been in a moment of envious rage, and besides, she was just a stupid kid then. She hadn't thought about the consequences of letting her sister tumble down those jagged, bone-breaking rocks. At the time, all she'd wanted was revenge and to keep Abby's mouth shut. She'd regretted it almost immediately and it had haunted Lori her entire life. She couldn't muster the nerve to commit murder. It just wasn't in her blood.

EIGHTEEN

LORI,

When I was a kid my uncle Zeke was like my best friend. He the one who done taught me the important stuff. Taught me how to use a gun and skin a deer. Taught me bout tools an moonshine an women.

Ya ask me why Asian women. That's cause a Zeke.

He done went to Vietnam. Mama always say he werent never the same after that. He talked to me a lot bout his time over there. Said he were scared at first but learned to have fun killin the gooks. Said it was like fuckin. Once you kill one you cant wait to kill another. Ha ha.

Showed me pictures hed developed himself of he an some other soldger rapin gook women, some of em just kids. Twas the first porn I ever saw an he let me borrow em. Showed me pictures of what he an his buddy done to them gooks when they was done fuckin em too. Pictures of my uncle stabbin an torturin them skinny bitches, rippin off they tits while theys were still alive. Cuttin out the pussy. In them pictures he was grinnin like a kid at Disneyland. Looked happier than I ever seen him in real life.

There were these other pictures he had of dead gooks stacked in piles and set on fire and shit. Villages burnin. Chopped off heads on sticks and body parts thrown everywheres. Even had pictures of him fuckin some a them dead heads. Let me borrow em too.

I didn't have no nudie magazeens. Zeke done told me they aint no good noways. Said his pictures were better cause in Playboy they dont show the good stuff. And when I finally done saw a nudie mag I saw just how right he was. Theys borin. They don't let ya see INSIDE the woman. Uncle Zekes pictures let ya see everythin.

When I was a youngin the only naked ladies I saw were them fuckin gooks, an they were gettin raped and murdered in every one. Docs say it gave me a fetish. I dont want no blond or redhead. I want dark hair and tiny bodies and slanty eyeballs. And I wanna do em just like Uncle Zeke done showed me.

One day Zeke gets put up in the loony bin after shootin his girlfrien in the head with a shotgun. Blew 1 whole half of her face away. I know cause I saw it. We were smokin meat out back a his river shack an they got to arguin bout somethin. Dont member what. Dont fuckin matter. What matters is I done cum in my pants when he shot her without even havin to touch myself. It was sexy an it was beautifull. I member cheerin when he did it too, like I was atta rock show. Didn't feel scared not at all. Knew he wouldn't hurt me none. He loved me like a lil brother. An I loved him too even though he were a man.

They wouldnt let me see him in the nuthouse. An they never done let him out. He died up in there. Peacefull. In his sleep. Probably havin sweet dreams of rapin and killin slanty eye cunts in the war. Like a real man.

I hope hes watchin over me now. Hope hes real proud of all I done.

Edmund

NINETEEN

THERE WAS A SLAPPING SOUND, like a tire on wet gravel, followed by a wobbling noise like a piece of tin being shook. Then there were chords, strings plucking. The acoustics reverberated off the walls of the mountains like bad dreams.

A slide guitar.

Even above the roar of the river, Lori could make out the distinct sound of it. The song was bluesy—slippery and rich with sinister undertones. There was menace to the melody, the notes deliberately haunting. This wasn't the slick, polished blues of Chicago, but dirty, raw, Southern blues, the kind Buzz had played, the only music Lori had been able to tune in on the radio once they'd arrived in Killen.

Lori looked to the stern of the boat. Hadn't Buzz's guitar been there a moment ago? She couldn't remember it going overboard, but it must have at some point, either during the fight or when she and Abby had disposed of the body. Had someone found the guitar? Maybe the kid who was running around in the woods, the one who'd almost convinced her, for a moment anyway, that he was Pete. But he had to be miles behind them by now. No, it made more sense that this was a different guitar, and someone else was out there playing it.

Then there was a voice. The singing was a wordless moan, filled with despair. The vocals fit this guitar's death dirge perfectly, deep with bass and as powerful as an avalanche, making Lori's skin prickle. She'd never heard anything like it before. She looked up, following the sound.

That's when she saw the shack.

It sat atop a wooded cliff that hung out over the river like a scythe, a dark country hovel silhouetted against the hellscape. Black smoke emanated from a crooked pipe on the roof. Someone was home.

Lori hit the motor. The current was strong here, pulling the boat upriver, but she wanted to get there as quickly as possible. The bloody water spread out behind them like a great, open wound. Particles of organic matter floated in this section of the river, chunks of what looked like torn meat. Lori tried not to look at them for fear she would identify something as human—a finger, a foot, a head or . . .

Lori suddenly wondered if she had gone mad. She felt as if she'd crossed over into another dimension of horror and pain. Had she died and gone to hell without realizing it? Had she been sent somewhere to suffer for all the rotten things she'd done? She didn't believe in the afterlife and had never been superstitious. But she'd also never experienced anything like this. The Hollow River existed in its own unnerving universe, and The River Man was the sun at its center.

Finding a safe shoreline to dock, Lori shut off the motor and lifted it on its hinges before guiding the bow into the sand. She couldn't get them too close to the cliff because there was no shore there, only rows of pointed rocks lined up like giant, black shark teeth. They would have to journey through the woods. If Abby couldn't make the uphill trek, she could stay behind with the boat. Lori didn't really care either way. Right now all that mattered was getting to the shack. She felt with utter certainty that she had found

GONE TO SEE THE RIVER MAN

The River Man at last. If she got the key to him, maybe it wouldn't matter that she hadn't killed Buzz. Handing over the key had to be the most important thing. It was the whole fucking purpose of this ordeal.

"We're gonna have to go up this hill," she told her sister. "It looks steep. Maybe you should stay behind."

Abby's face soured. "I wanna see The River Man, Sissy."

"It's all rock and brush. You can't really use your crutches."

"I can do it. I'm not the little kid you think you made me into."

Abby's words made Lori turn away, unable to look her in the eye. "Alright. Let's get going then. It'll be dark soon."

They secured the boat, looping the rope around a white willow tree that jutted out over the riverbank. It was pink in this world and its knots looked like sores. When she looked closer, Lori realized the knots were bleeding. She glanced at the surrounding woods. Blood trickled from dead branches and seeped through the cracks between the rocks. Lori shuddered but would not retreat.

Not knowing how long they'd be gone or what they might need, they gathered their backpacks, Lori clipping the mace to her belt. Abby left her crutches behind, as if to prove a point, but Lori strapped them to her own pack before putting it over her shoulders. If nothing else, she wasn't going to leave behind a murder weapon.

Entering the woods was the easy part. Here there was only packed dirt and dying brush. But onward was a rocky, mountainous terrain riddled with fallen trees and debris. No trails in sight, just dense, unforgiving thicket. Here the woods were more black than red and so cold a coating of frost had formed upon the branches. Behind the sisters, the boat rocked in the blood as if waving goodbye, as if they were going to a place from which they may never return.

•••

To Lori's surprise, Abby was managing to scramble up the rocks, but was crouched over so she could use her hands too. This made the journey much slower than if Lori had gone on her own. There was no avoiding it now—they would be on the river past nightfall, if nightfall ever came in this red dimension. She might miss work tomorrow. She'd only taken two days off from her regular six-days-a-week schedule. And with Killen offering little to no cellular service, she wouldn't even be able to call out sick. They had no shelter if it rained again—*would it rain blood?*—and worse yet, they were running out of food.

Lori stood at the top of the rock clusters, gazing down at Abby. Her sister's body was taut with struggle, but her face showed no signs of stress. She seemed distant, as if her mind was completely detached from what her body was doing.

I never should have brought her along. I should have found a babysitter. She says she's not a kid, but that's exactly what she is. Can't leave her alone, always needs me to watch over her to make sure she doesn't fall down or stick her tongue in a wall socket. I can never go anywhere because of her. No wonder I searched for a pen pal. I haven't been able to take vacations or even go out on dates. Even going to work is difficult because of her.

For years Lori had felt guilty about ruining Abby's life, but as she'd gotten older it had become clear that Abby had ruined Lori's life in return. This was where Lori's irritation with her truly began to fester. She often wondered what it would have been like if Abby hadn't survived that fall. Would the guilt have eaten away at her, just as the guilt of incest had eaten away at Pete? Or would she get over it easier without having Abby around as a constant reminder of what she'd done? Would being able to have a life of her own compensate for eternal guilt?

"Hurry up," Lori snapped.

"I'm comin', Sissy."

Abby pulled herself over another boulder, but her right foot slipped and she nearly tumbled before hugging the rock. Lori didn't even flinch.

"This is why I told you to stay with the fucking boat."

"I can do it, Sissy."

"You're gonna take all damn night."

"I said *I can do it*!"

Lori surprised herself by laughing. It just felt so good to be better than Abby at something. All these years she'd been capable of doing things her sister couldn't—walk, talk and think among them—and yet she'd been so clouded by guilt she'd failed to really realize her superiority. The power had shifted years ago. Why did she so often let herself, and perhaps even Abby, think they still held the same older sister dynamic they'd had before the great fall? Was Lori that traumatized by how Abby had hurt her and stolen David from her, always besting her when they were kids?

She laughed now, because it was worthy of laughter. Abby was a crippled mongoloid, friendless and unfuckable. Lori would be better than her for the rest of their lives. Abby could never take Edmund from her now, no matter how many people she killed. The danger had seemed so real earlier today; now it seemed like a total absurdity.

"Stop laughing at me, Sissy! I'm almost there!"

But Lori couldn't help it; hell, she didn't want to. It wasn't until Abby had reached the top of the hill that Lori's laughter tapered off to giggles. Abby got to her feet on her own without asking for her sister's help as she normally would have, and Lori simply didn't care. Given Abby's behavior throughout this trip, she expected her to say something hurtful, but her sister seemed too winded to do so. She hunched over, arms curled and wrists limp. Her legs bowed inward in an hourglass.

You're pathetic, Lori thought. But she didn't say it. The laughter had said enough for now. Abby's behavior had changed since they'd been in these woods. Lori told herself her own changes of heart were unrelated, that she wasn't being affected by where they were. But it was a hard sell. That didn't matter, though. Her thoughts toward her sister were entirely justified. They'd always been there, but were suppressed by a guilt she'd now begun to think she never should have felt in the first place.

There was a rustle in the bushes. The sisters scanned the woods, Lori reaching for the mace at her belt. There was another rustle and the thicket just above them swayed. Lori's heart filled her throat as the pale feet appeared again, her dead brother's laughter coming with it.

Abby beamed. "Petey!"

She began scrambling up the incline, a wide smile on her face. For the first time that day she was her old self again, the childlike Abby she'd been all of her adult life.

"Abby, wait!"

But her sister wasn't listening. She was too excited. "Petey, I missed you so much!"

The feet vanished into the woods again, pale flesh swallowed by the blackness of the mountain.

"Abby, it's not . . . not . . ." She still couldn't even bring herself to say his name. "We don't know who that is!"

Abby glanced back at her, confused. "Petey's our brother, Sissy. Don't you remember him?"

"It's not *him*. It can't be him. He's . . . he's dead."

"But that's what I wanted."

Lori blinked. "What?"

"My wish! I haven't even told The River Man what my wish is yet, but he already granted it!"

"Wish? No, Abby, he's not, like, a genie in a bottle. He's a . . . he's . . ."

But she didn't know.

"I wished for Petey. I miss him, Sissy. Don't you miss him?"

Lori nodded but didn't speak. An all too familiar sting was festering in her chest like pus.

There was another rustle, closer this time, louder, the sounds of tree branches being snapped away. The boyish laughter returned, then the voice spoke.

"You're gonna get hurt!"

It was Pete's voice. He wasn't threatening, he seemed as if he were trying to warn them.

Abby huffed. "For God's sake, Pete, don't be a wussy."

That summer day so long ago came rushing back to Lori, a distant memory resurrected in full color. It was on that day Lori first noticed how fragile her brother could be, and she would later take advantage of that fragility, time and again.

"No!" her brother shouted from the bushes. "I'm not doing it!"

Abby turned to her, eyes like open graves. "Lori! Put him on the swing and push him over!"

Lori couldn't believe it. Abby seemed to remember her every word from that day, and the figure in the woods was feeding her Pete's lines right back, recreating their childhood in a macabre play.

"Show yourself!" Lori's voiced echoed up the mountain. "If you're our brother, show yourself!"

More laughter. "You're gonna get hurt, Lori!"

This time it *was* a threat.

"You're gonna get *real* hurt!" he said. "It's your turn, Lori! Your turn!"

Abby started clapping, giddy in her applause.

"You're not our fucking brother!" Lori shouted, hoping to convince herself. "Our brother is *dead*!"

"We can't keep doing this. It's wrong, Lori. It's wrong."

"Shut up!" she gritted her teeth against the rising tears. "Just shut up!"

"I'm . . . I dunno . . . *scared*."

She put her hands over her ears. "Shut your fucking mouth!"

"We have to stop!"

Lori charged into the brush toward the voice. She crashed through a tangle of thorn bushes and they pulled at her clothes, stalling her as the white shape slipped between the trees like mist.

The body was lithe, but human—naked. His ribs were showing, hips jutting out like bullhorns. He was not just skinny; he was emaciated. The boy turned to look at Lori only once, then disappeared into a black curtain of shadows, red mist drifting where he'd stood a moment ago.

"It's not my fault," she whispered.

But that wasn't true.

Not at all.

TWENTY

PETE'S EYES HAD SUNK INTO his skull. Blue veins stood out on his pale skin. He'd withered into a scarecrow of his former self, and the feeding tubes had only helped to prolong his self-imposed deterioration, forcing artificial nutrition into him that made him shit liquid several times a day. And whenever he wasn't being watched, he took the tube out.

"He's burrowed deep inside himself," Dr. Thompson told Mom and Dad.

He was the new psychiatrist, one who specialized in troubled teens with eating disorders. Seeing the regular therapist hadn't produced any results or even revealed what was wrong with Pete, so now they were approaching psychiatric drugs, when they could get Pete to ingest them.

Mom wasn't sobbing anymore. The past couple of months she'd cried a flood. Now it seemed her reserves had run dry. She only stared off blankly like a mannequin while Dad did all the talking, and in a weird way it made Lori wish her mother would start bawling again. Anything was better than this zombie state.

"Has he told you anything?" Dad asked. "Anything at all?"

Lori hadn't forced Pete into sex in weeks. He was too sick for one thing, but she'd also been feeling terrible remorse, not just for what she'd done to him, but for what she'd done to their sister. It seemed so unfair that her parents should have two children in the hospital at the same time, one recovering from a near death experience, the other dancing with death.

Abby was permanently fractured, mentally as well as bodily, but not being fully aware of all she had lost in the fall, she was often in high spirits. The daughter they'd known and loved was gone, but her positivity at least made it easier for Mom and Dad to be around her.

Pete, on the other hand, was trapped under a black cloud, one Lori knew was comprised of shame and fear that he never shared. He'd simply given up on life and was ending his in the most agonizing way possible for himself and everyone who loved him. It was hard for Lori not to hate him for it, and she wondered if her parents felt that same hatred.

What Pete's doing is selfish! He's taken this anorexic crap way too far.

So weeks before he was admitted into the hospital, she'd stopped forcing him to have sex. He'd gotten what he wanted. She'd backed off completely. Why wasn't that enough? Why did he have to keep punishing the whole family just to get back at her?

Because he's the youngest, the baby. He always gets all the pampering, and Abby gets all the freedom while middle child Lori is forgotten in the shuffle.

She shifted in the hard, plastic chair and crossed her arms. Dad noted her frustration and excused himself from the doctor. He took out his wallet and gave her five dollars.

"Honey, why don't you go on down to the cafeteria and get yourself a little something." He forced a smile, then seemed to think better of it. He handed her another five. "Pick out something from the gift shop too."

Lori got up. "Thanks, Dad."

She slipped out of the room and stepped into the glaring, fluorescent hallway. It smelled of sanitizer and riboflavin, of old ladies and urine. All around her, machines beeped softly. Nurses in blue

GONE TO SEE THE RIVER MAN

pajamas paid her no attention as she headed toward the elevator, thinking of the magazines and candy and trinkets she'd eyed at the gift shop earlier. She thought of buying something for Abby, if only to continue to divert any suspicion, but decided she wanted the laser pointer keychain more, even though she had no real use for it. Maybe she could get a kitten to drive crazy with it. Her siblings were getting the most attention from Mom and Dad, but Lori was getting spillover sympathy and concern, so a kitten might not be out of the question. Her parents asked about her emotional state but were too busy with their own to spend time on hers. At least Dad kept giving her cash. Sometimes she felt guilty for taking it, though she wasn't sure why, but it was nice to have money to piss away. She was a teenager, after all. It was in her blood to shop. The thought made her chuckle and a nurse with a hard face glanced at her. Lori felt instantly guilty and stared at her feet.

She had to pass by the physical therapy ward to get to the elevator. She spotted her sister through the long wall of windows separating the exercise room from the hall. It was bright in there too, but it was sunlight, gentle and golden, unlike the harsh light of the halls. Abby was on a sort of runway with support bars on either side, trying to walk but failing as an overweight orderly helped her along. For all the bolts that had gone into them, Abby's legs seemed totally useless. Her head was wrapped in fresh caster, making her look bald and bulbous, but at least it hid some of her stitches. Her face was pink from straining and the orderly was reminding her not to hold her breath.

Watching the mangled remains of her sister struggling to learn the basics of life all over again, it occurred to Lori that David had not come to visit.

•••

They cremated Pete two days before Christmas.

It was the first day Abby had left the hospital since her fall. She was still in a wheelchair, but she'd gotten so she could take herself to the bathroom. Her recovery was slow, but progress had been made, and there was hope she would walk again. Mom said it was the one Christmas miracle they got that year. Lori wasn't sure which way to take that but was happy to hear Mom say anything at all.

They'd held a funeral earlier in the week. Family, friends and distant relatives Lori had only seen at weddings came back into their lives for one grievous day, then vanished again, leaving a table of casseroles, lasagnas and greeting cards in their wake. Lots of flowers to wither and die. But only the immediate family was present for the scattering of the ashes.

Dad tried to say a few words but choked on grief. Mom stared off into the woods, drugged by a sadness that would prove to never end. Abby had fallen somber along with the rest of the family but didn't seem to know what was going on.

Wanting to ease her father's suffering, Lori took the urn from him.

"Goodbye, Pete. We love you."

She tossed her brother out over the creek where they'd used to swing out, sail through the air, and swim and play in the summer sun.

TWENTY-ONE

A MEATY ODOR WAFTED DOWN from between the trees. They were dead up here, their branches curling down like witch fingers, blood icicles their long nails. The smell was like that of cooking beef except foul, as if sulfur and feces had been thrown into the mix. Lori thought of the smoke she'd seen emanating from the shack, sure that's where the scent was coming from.

What's he cooking in there?

Her mind flashed with sick images—a human arm being grated like cheese, a string of crisp guts draped over a fire, an aborted fetus bobbing in a stew. As quickly as the thoughts came, Lori shook them out of her head, mortified by her own imagination. Had her brain gone dark? Was she truly going insane?

Her thighs were burning from the hike. It was amazing Abby had been able to continue. But the woods thinned as they struggled up the incline, giving way to a skinny trail. There were no signs or arrows, no warnings to keep out, but the dark knots in the white birch trees seemed like screaming faces to her now, the poltergeists of those who'd died in agony, suggesting she should abandon hope if she entered.

She stopped, telling herself it was to catch her breath, and Abby stopped behind her.

"Almost there, Sissy."

"Almost."

"I'll bet that's where Petey is. Up there in The River Man's house."

Lori didn't reply. She grabbed the canteen from her bag and took a drink. Her mouth held a bitter taste. Even the water had the flavor of coins. Her body ached, she felt lightheaded, and she was so very cold. The sky was a darker shade of red now, dusk falling in a plume that would rot to black. She wondered what time it was, but somehow knew such a thing had no meaning here. This was a place beyond time, beyond the rules of Earth. Perhaps The River Man was too.

They moved on, across grass turned black as ash, through a grove of trees curling out of the dirt like a warped ribcage. There were no birds, no squirrels. No cicadas clicked. No frogs croaked. Lori and Abby were the only signs of life.

Except for Pete, Lori thought. *Or something posing as Pete.*

One guess made as little sense as the other, and oddly enough she was getting used to the confusion. The visions or hallucinations or whatever they were had become commonplace. Real or imagined, Lori accepted them without flinching. Madness was an afterthought. What mattered first and foremost was getting to the shack and handing over the damned key. She didn't just want it done to please Edmund and get on home. She wanted to see The River Man now, in the flesh. Maybe then this would all make sense, but certainly not before. Maybe never.

A familiar voice called out of the shadows. A man's, but not Pete's.

"Daddy done made a deal . . ."

Lori turned about, unsure where the voice was coming from. It seemed to be everywhere and nowhere.

"I ain't told ya it all."

Buzz.

GONE TO SEE THE RIVER MAN

She looked to Abby but her sister seemed unfazed. Her face was slack, eyes vacant. If anything, she looked like she was daydreaming. Lori scanned the woods again. They were so thin here, and the voice was so clear, as if the dead man was fast approaching.

But is he really dead? He has to be . . .

"Daddy wanted to be a bluesman," the voice said. "He could play guitar like his fingers were made of lightnin', but it weren't enough for him noways. So he went on to see The River Man. Didn't come back for a long time, but when he done did, he played guitar like nothin' you ever heard before. He come back with a gift, but also come back mean as a rattlesnake. He beat up on us now, and when Mama tried to stop him, he done whipped her worst of all."

There was a crackling in the woods behind them. Lori spun, not sure if she wanted to see him or not, not sure of anything. Buzz was partly hidden behind a birch that should have been too thin to conceal even half his body. He had gone coal black, but the blood trickling down his forehead was bright and clear. Other than the whites of his eyes, the redness of the blood was his only color. Even his clothes had gone black.

"Daddy took to the stage like an animal. Crowds loved him. He started sleepin' with tramps who'd do anythin' for a man who could make a guitar wail and hum like Daddy did."

Lori took her sister's arm. "Do you see him?"

Abby sighed in her waking coma.

"Abby?"

"But it weren't enough," Buzz went on. "Not the women, the booze or the music. Daddy wanted fame and money. Coulda got 'em too, being that good. Instead he got famous 'round here for somethin' else."

Lori's mouth was dry again, but she didn't reach for her canteen. Her hand was locked beside the mace canister at her hip, though it now gave her no sense of security. She wanted to keep on walking but dared not move. She doubted Buzz would let her go without finishing his story. And in a way, she felt she owed him that much.

"First he done killed a man over a woman; not Mama, but one of them tramps. 'Twas her husband, but Daddy didn't take no mind. Said she was his now and that was that. So the husband comes to Daddy's show and gets up on stage with a knife. Daddy got cut up somethin' terrible, but he got the knife away from that man someways and done stuck him in the gut. Stuck him fifteen times.

"That's what The River Man do. He ain't gotta ask ya to do nothin' evil. He just bring out the evil that's *already in ya*. Daddy went on to jail that night, but they had to let him go in the mornin' 'cause it be self-defense. If they'd done kept him in a cage like he belonged, he never woulda got no chance to do what he did to us."

The nature of this story caused Lori to turn to her sister, but Abby wasn't there. Lori's spine went hard as she scanned the woods. She was alone—alone but for the ghost of Buzz Fledderjohn.

"Abby?" she whispered, too afraid to raise her voice.

Blood sluiced through Buzz's teeth.

"Daddy was beatin' on me when it happened. I done stained the sofa eatin' huckleberries and he was goin' at me with a switch. I was hollerin', beggin' him to stop 'cause he was makin' me bleed. But he just kept on whoopin' me. Mama tried to stop him, and he punched her in the belly so hard she fell over. So she went on into the kitchen—come back with a fryin' pan. She beat on him good before he was able to get it away from her, just like he got that man's knife. And he goes an' does the same thing with that pan, crushing my Mama's skull right before my eyes."

With those final words, the trickle of blood on Buzz's forehead was drowned out by a sudden gush of it. His skull split apart, releasing a hot stream that ran down his face and chest, blood sousing him, mutilated brains splattering about his shoulders like stew.

Lori screamed and covered her eyes.

GONE TO SEE THE RIVER MAN

"Sissy?"

A hand fell on her back. Lori jolted and opened wide her eyes, shaking.

"Don't be scared, Sissy. It's just me."

Abby was rubbing Lori's back, making little circles just like their mother had when she was trying to get the children to sleep. Lori held her sister close and scanned the thicket. They were alone in the dark, crimson woods.

"Did . . . did you see him?"

Abby whispered, a child telling a secret. "They're all here, Sissy. Here with us."

Something went cold and damp within Lori, as if seeping through her clothes. Stepping away from Abby, she saw what her sister was holding in her free hand. Lori gagged.

Buzz's foot was slick with gore. Abby fingered the fractured bone jutting from the stump and petted the ripped flesh, smiling as if it were her birthday.

"For luck, Sissy."

Behind her there was only darkness in the east. Night was swallowing them, and the fear of being lost in these woods after dark was sinking in deeper. How many ghosts would haunt her once the sun had deserted them? How many old demons would surface? Would it get cold enough to freeze to death? How would they find their way without tripping over rocks and branches on the way down?

She didn't tell Abby to get rid of the foot and didn't ask how she'd gotten it. She doubted her sister would even know. All that mattered was pressing on.

"Let's go," she said. "It's growing dark."

• • •

The shack was windowless. The last red sliver on the horizon silhouetted it in a Halloween glow. Lori could just make it out from the trail. They were only a hundred yards or so below it now. She could scarcely believe they'd finally arrived. The smell of burning animal flesh was as thick as the smoke billowing from the chimney in a black rainbow, flowing with the same rage as the river. They were near the edge of the cliff, the waters slamming against the rocks below, the sound as sharp as if she were swimming in it.

Abby whispered. "That's where he lives, right, Sissy?"

Lori nodded, unable to speak, dread melding with a sense of wonder. She was unlocking something here, decoding some ancient dream. Perhaps that was the true meaning of the key she'd dug out of the dead woman's chest. That gruesome excavation seemed so long ago now. It was jumbled in the mud of bad memories, just another shit stain on her soul. A mangled life of misery had led her to this abyss, every choice and step bringing her closer to this cliff, this jagged edge of insanity. And she held the key. After decades of helpless pain, Lori was finally in control. She had pushed herself in an unrelenting quest for what she wanted, what she needed. She had earned it—earned *him*. This crooked country shack was the last stop on a journey through her own soul, and when she emerged from it she would not be the Lori she knew and hated. This doorway was a birth canal of splintered wood. She would be resurrected from the rot and cinders she'd made of her life and would at long last be happy.

There would be joy. There would be light. There would be love.

Edmund.

Her heart grew warm. The world saw Edmund as a beast, just as they would see her as one if anyone knew her secrets. The truth *does* hurt. Truth is pain—sharp and deep and merciless. Only love can ease the suffering, for love is the sharing of those truths. There was catharsis there, deep in the soft, pink belly of tenderness. She'd never told anyone what she'd told Edmund. That's how she knew he was the one, the embracer of her most private evils.

"Gonna see The River Man," Abby said.

Lori awoke from her reverie, but the world around her was even more surreal than the one she kept within. The trees were larger here, decayed branches running across a burgundy sky in pulsing, black veins. They seemed to be breathing. Lori's eyes locked on the cabin so tightly she forgot to blink. They watered and burned but refused to close. She was suddenly afraid that she would blink the shack out of existence and awaken to find her life was the stale, gray ruin it had always been, so she let the tears fall as they approached the withered abode.

The shack leaned forward, a suicide jumper inching over the cliff. Low fog created by the chimney smoke hid the ground around it, writhing at the sisters' feet like a bed of snakes. They inched closer, side by side, neither sister the leader now. Lori walked a little faster. This was her quest. Abby wouldn't upstage her this time; she wouldn't allow it. When they reached the door, Lori moved in front of her, but hesitated to knock.

Hanging from the roof were small, blackened bones and bird feathers, wreaths made from old guitar strings. Dead locusts and field mice were scattered before the entryway like gifts. Unfamiliar symbols had been carved into the shack's wood—moons and stars inside of diamonds, mountain lions with pentagram heads—and upon the door hung the mighty skull of a creature Lori could not identify. It almost looked like the remains of some sort of dinosaur or other prehistoric beast. Small lines had been painted across the bone, a makeshift map of sorts—*a map of the river*, she realized. Below the skull, in the dead center of the door, was a keyhole. No doorknob or knocker, just a rusted slot.

Reaching for the key, Lori realized it was already in her hand. She wondered how long she'd been carrying it. It was no longer metallic, but hard, organic matter. Cartilage. Dehydrated sinew. She dared not look at it for fear it would reveal something that would make her withdraw from the doorstep and the quest altogether. The key slid into the lock, old bodies in the act of love. The lock turned, sounding like a popping vertebra, and the door inched open, mucus peeling away from its frame. The boards swelled with stale air and breathed hot pus.

First there was the smell of death—rot combined with the burning meat odor Lori had caught while on the mountain. In the crack between the door and frame was a flickering glow that tossed the shadows. She placed one hand on the oozing door—fingertips only—and nudged. She stepped in the doorway for a closer look, and then the world gave way to a deep, freezing abyss. Here there was only darkness, a blind realm sporadically splintered by tongues of blood-red flame.

There was no air to scream with.

All Lori could do was fall.

Helpless.

Alone.

TWENTY-TWO

SHE WAS IN A POOL, nude, floating on her back with her arms and legs splayed out, her body in the shape of a star. Even with her eyes closed, Lori could tell there was light here. She could see it through eyelids she was hesitant to open. She remembered falling, but not landing or splashing into whatever she was drifting in. The water didn't move like the river, but somehow she knew she was in the river. Perhaps this dead pool was where the river ended. Would this be blood too? The water was certainly warm enough.

She opened her eyes. Above her was a galaxy of red stars, a thousand needle holes poked through black velvet, giving a glimpse of a brighter world beyond. There was a low hum, like an out of tune guitar played through a blown amplifier, and the vibrations it caused rippled through the water and tickled awake her flesh like the fingertips of a man. She thought of Edmund, of David and Matt and the line of nobodies that had never lasted.

And then she thought of her brother.

Her vagina grew moist, nipples hardening. But she wasn't craving a fuck. She wanted to be caressed. She wanted to be kissed and touched and have tender foreplay with all the men she'd ever gone to bed with, all at once, to be the center of a passionate orgy where she would be worshipped as a goddess.

As quickly as the desire came upon her it vanished, replaced by hunger and thirst. Lori wanted rare steak and vodka. She wanted a Thanksgiving feast. Another need arose. She wanted strength now, power and influence, the ability to lead and control people. The desire to dominate was raw and savage, a craving she'd never fully been aware of. But she had dominated Pete and loved it. And in crippling her sister, Lori had become dominant over Abby. Where sibling rivalry was concerned, she had proven herself champion. And she fucking loved it. But outside of her own kin, she had always been submissive, even weak.

There was only one person she should ever submit to. She knew that now. A woman should only bow at the feet of her king, a man worthy of possessing her. She had found her king, but he was behind bars. All of humanity fought to keep her from the one thing that would take the pain away. The world wanted her to die alone without having ever known pure love. And as the cravings came and went, toppling over one another, one wish remained where it had risen, refusing to yield to the next. It was strong enough to keep her from sinking into the rising blood all about her, intense enough to widen every pinhole in the darkness, letting the crimson light grow stronger until the black barrier tore apart.

Lori rose from the pool, walking upon the surface of the water like a gore-slathered Christ. With each step she left another footprint of pink flame as she merged with this dimension, its raw energy pumping through her pores. Her skeleton shook against the meat that struggled to contain her spirit. Her organs writhed, awoke, her heart going still as a corpse's only to thunder back to life.

The humming sound had blossomed. There was strumming now, low and deep and merciless. An electric slide guitar, droning doom-wrought blues. Churning through the light were the faces of animals not of earthbound origin—mutants, monsters, demons. They roared silent screams, eyes burning, jaws gleaming. And in the center of the light a shadow emerged, tall and lean, a vision layered

GONE TO SEE THE RIVER MAN

upon a cosmic hell of visions.

The sudden change in light made Lori gasp. She'd almost forgotten the color blue. There was no transition through purple. The red became a tornado and spiraled into a moonlight glow, reflecting off the guitar in the tall figure's hands. As the light spread, the man's hands came into view, and Lori winced at the sight of them. Not only were there thumbs on each side of the hands, giving the player four altogether, but there were five fingers between those thumbs, curled and arthritic, and yet they strummed and plucked with ease. The palms and backsides of both hands were covered in fingernails that sprouted out of his coal-black flesh like horns.

The man stood where he played, letting Lori approach. With every step she took, more of him was revealed to her. A huge, untamed briar of gray hair rose from his skull, matching a beard that served as a hive. The man seemed unbothered by the wasps and worms ducking in and out of it. Braids hung from his chin, knotted off with chicken bones and crow feathers. His dark face was scaly. His eyes were sunken, red where they should have been white, and his teeth were jagged, matching the rocks of the Hollow River. A skeletal body with clothes molded and rotted, a trench coat covered in patches, rips and dust, spider webs clinging to the shoulders as though he'd just dug his way out of the grave.

He played on, singing without words. They were guttural moans—raspy, mean. His throat clicked and his fangs chattered in percussion, perfectly timed to his guitar work, a hissing one-man-band.

When she was merely a foot away, Lori stopped. She might have gotten down on her knees like a child praying had it not been for her revelation that only Edmund was worth bowing to. Instead she waited—for what she did not know—listening to the ominous blues that belted out of this towering scarecrow. The man's music needed no lyrics. It was all there in his moans and clicks and grunts, and his fingers said more through the guitar than words ever could. In these haunting blues, Lori felt every bit of suffering she'd endured. She felt somehow cleansed by it, each note another teardrop held back too long. It was as if this was her own personal dirge, a ballad composed of her deepest, most secret pains.

That's what he wants, she realized. *The pain of others. Our suffering. Our heartache and regrets. Our grief and fear. All so his music can be unflinching and true, raw as road-rash flesh.*

Every note he plays is a drop of blood from someone's heart.

The man's head swayed side to side, lost in the bliss of Lori's suffering.

She struggled to speak. "Are you . . ."

The fingernails on his palms twitched, the guitar floating into a distorted riff more common to heavy metal. Lori listened. Waited. The solo slid off into a drone, the man's hands moving away from the strings. The dull hum returned. Lori's song was over, for now.

"You're The River Man. I know you're him. The man I love sent me to find you. To give you that key."

The River Man only nodded.

"But that's not what I'm really giving you, is it?"

He smiled. A crocodile. A possum. "Surely there can be no question about that now."

"Do you, um . . . do you know me?"

"You are the woman that belongs to Edmund. The Willing One."

She gulped. "My name is Lori."

"Your name doesn't matter. What matters is the pain, and you, darling, are dripping in it."

"Maybe you can take some of it away."

He snorted a laugh. "Not exactly. But I do make deals."

"Okay." She crossed her arms, aware of her nudity and the vulnerability it presented. "What do you want from me?"

"Nothing you don't want yourself."

"I think I finally know what that is. I want Edmund by my side.

GONE TO SEE THE RIVER MAN

It's clear as day to me now. I don't want to love him through a set of bars for the rest of our lives."

The River Man's eyes flashed. "And yet you know the man is a vicious murderer who brutally slaughters women."

"He's just a misunderstood soul."

"Like you."

"*Exactly* like me. That's why we're so right for each other."

The River Man leaned in, his dark face curling. "And you are certain about that?"

Lori swallowed hard. "What do you mean? Of course I'm certain."

"You've made a lot of big decisions in your life, Lori. Can you say that even half of them worked out for the best?"

She looked away, unable to face him, unable to face herself. But this wasn't one of those poor decisions. She'd grown and learned so much. She knew what was right for her, even if she'd been wrong so many times before.

"I just want love," she said. "That's all I've ever wanted."

"Indeed. Physical love you took from your brother. Secret love you felt for David. Unrequited love for Matthew. With each one, things went wrong. Love grew just enough to have an impactful death."

Lori hugged herself, head down. "That wasn't my fault."

"Of course not. There was always an obstacle. Always *the same* obstacle. Wasn't there?"

Her fists balled. "She didn't . . ."

"Oh, but she did. First she stole David from you before you'd even shared a single kiss with him. Then she stopped you from perfecting your lovemaking skills with Pete. And because you had to spend so much time taking care of her, you couldn't give your relationship with Matthew the effort it needed to flourish. Instead it withered away, leaving you alone again, always alone."

The River Man's bitter truths were sharper than his teeth. Lori curled inward, unable to look him in the eye. *Those crimson eyes.*

"Now you're trying to gain Edmund's love by coming up my river. You've found me, whereas so many others gave up searching before coming anywhere near this shack. Edmund found me too. You think that makes you kindred spirits. Maybe you think that makes you worthy of his affection. But whether you're meant to be together or not, there's still those bars between you, those walls—that same old *obstacle*."

Lori looked at him. He had regressed into shadow, the blue light fading, a black cloud passing across the face of the moon.

"Only you can tear down the walls," he said. "You must destroy the obstacle to free Edmund, and free yourself."

Lori nodded. "So what do I do?"

His smile was all she could see.

"You finish what you started, Lori," he said. "You finish what you started."

•••

When Lori entered the shack, she collapsed almost instantly. Abby gasped, dropping Buzz's foot, and ran inside.

"Sissy?"

An odor hit her like a sucker punch. Coughing, she put her hand over her nose and mouth, and looked all around. The walls of the shack were lined with drying strips of flesh. On its own, the door closed behind her, but she was too worried about her sister to notice.

Sissy was everything. Abby had been dependent on her for so long. The sudden thought of losing her was a fear she couldn't process. It was too heavy, too complex. And as Abby's mind went dark, the shack went darker, illuminated only by a wood-burning stove in the corner, its flames revealing a shadowy figure propped up in a rocking chair beside it.

Abby got on her knees beside her sister and tapped her cheeks.

"Sissy? Sissy wake up!"

GONE TO SEE THE RIVER MAN

Lori remained lifeless. Tears welled in Abby's eyes. She took her sister by the arms and shook her to no avail.

"Sissy, please wake up!"

The rocking chair creaked. The silhouette shifted. Abby sensed it more than saw it. She was thinking more clearly than she was used to. When she tried to look, the figure blended into the shadows on the walls, but she knew it was there, that *he* was there.

"River Man," she said, "you gotta help us."

There was a breathy, lion's grumble from the corner that made Abby's skin quiver. The sound swelled with static, the organic nature of it fusing into an electric hum, a primal scream becoming the heavy drone of a guitar. It grew louder as the shadowy figure inched forward, gliding more than walking, serpent-like.

When his warty face was revealed, Abby couldn't help but stare. His beard writhed with maggots and wasps, and when he smiled his teeth reflected the firelight in a sickly glow. His eyes told Abby something she couldn't put into words, but understood nonetheless.

"Where is she?" Abby asked.

"The river."

Abby furrowed her brow. "The river?"

"The one you traveled up today. The one you fell into on the day of your accident. The one your brother's remains were scattered into."

"Those are different rivers. One's the creek by Mommy and Daddy's house."

"No, my dear. There is but one river that runs through you and your sister's world. One river stained with blood. Blood shed by your sister. *Your* blood, Abby."

Abby winced. She didn't understand what he was saying, but she also didn't like it. She was suddenly wet from head to toe, her body swaying as if floating. In the corners of her eyes she saw jagged rocks speckled with blood. She shook her head and it all went away, but she could still feel a trace of it lingering. A loneliness she'd always feared burrowed its way inside her heart to feast.

"I wanna go home. Wake Sissy up so we can go home."

The River Man's breath came out in a fog. "She has chosen her journey. She's been on it her whole life."

Abby looked at Lori's slack, gray face and grabbed her sister's shirt in her fists, sniffling. All along their trip, Abby had slipped in and out of the world she knew and understood. It was as if she kept waking from repeating nightmares in which she felt only rage toward her sister, rage she could not remember the cause of but flamed within her nonetheless. Something had been whispering in her mind since they'd come to this valley, something as ancient as pain itself, and though her understanding of it was limited, she felt the evil of its presence, as clear and cold as winter rain.

"I wanna change my wish, River Man."

He didn't speak, only watched her, unblinking.

"I wanted Petey back. But he's dead. That's what he wanted, so I guess he's gotta be on your river. Me and Sissy don't. We don't wanna be on your river no more."

The River Man leaned over her, gazing down like some withered god. He gestured with his deformed body to the strips of flesh that curtained the walls. They gleamed with moisture, steaming in the cold—fresh cuts. The shack constricted. The stench of death burned in Abby's throat. She shuddered, knowing she was entombed in this place, a splintering shell of her own desperation, and when she closed her eyes she felt weightless. Wind gushed around her. She was falling. All she could hear was water crashing against rock, the sound growing louder and louder. When she tried to open her eyes again, the bones in her legs grinded and popped, and she closed them tighter as the pain came. It raked up her lower back, cracking her pelvis and twisting the vertebrae. Her face slammed into stones and her neck spun with a pop. When she was finally able to open her eyes, Abby was drenched, and no amount of blinking would take it away.

GONE TO SEE THE RIVER MAN

"Your sister's nature is toxicity," The River Man said. "This is why she seeks love in the arms of such evil. She and I are just about done in the river now. My song is almost over." He gave Abby a yellowed smile. "But what of you, my darling? You're so open, you've been feeling my touch long before you got here. It's been in your harsh words and fatal actions. So what does Abby *the big sister* want?"

She ran one hand over Lori's hair. "I want Sissy back. Gimmie my Sissy. That's all I want."

"Lori brought me the key. What have you to offer The River Man? I know you brought something for me."

Abby looked to the ceiling, as if it held answers. What did she have that she could give him? Her flashlight? The treats in her fanny pack? She didn't want to give up her stuffed doggy, Mongo, but would do it to save Sissy. What would The River Man like? Abby looked to him again, noticing the animal bones in his beard. Were they good luck charms, like her rabbit's foot? Would he like that?

Then it came to her.

"I do!" she said. "I do have something for you, River Man."

Abby didn't want to leave her sister alone in the shack with him, but she would make it quick, even though getting up from this position was always difficult. Struggling to her feet, she put her hand on the wall to brace herself. The strips of flesh oozed at her touch, and when she pulled away trails of red slime came with her fingers. The River Man did not help her rise, but the door to the shack opened on its own, revealing the black stranglehold of the night. A dusting of red stars made a blood-splatter of the cosmos, giving a faint but eerie glow to the cliff and mountains beyond. Abby clutched her arms against the chill of the breeze that rose from the river below. It sounded like a hurricane. It sounded *alive*.

Just outside the door was Buzz's severed foot. The meat was in the early stages of rigor mortis, the skin calloused and discolored. Blackish blood dribbled from the stump when Abby picked it up.

She turned around, cradling her offering like a new mother, and stepped back over the threshold. The door closed behind her again and The River Man stroked his beard, centipedes and black widows escaping into the fingernails that covered his hands. He gazed at the offering, smacking his lips.

"Ah, your trophy," he said. "The trophy you took from your victim."

Abby shook her head. "It's for good luck."

"Aren't they always?"

Abby didn't know. She just hoped he liked Buzz's foot enough to let her leave with Sissy. Without her, she would never make it home, and even if she did, home would never be the same without Sissy. She took care of all the things Abby couldn't.

Abby bit her lip just thinking about it. She could never make it on her own. It didn't matter what all the doctors and therapists tried to tell her. She *was* helpless. She *was* a retard. Without Sissy, she would die. And she truly loved her Sissy. Not just because she was her caretaker, but because she was her sister, her only living relative, her only friend. Abby would always protect her, just as she had when Buzz was attacking her. She'd killed him for trying to hurt Sissy.

A darkness had overtaken her in that moment, but she was grateful for it. The darkness had come and gone several times since they'd come out to these woods. Maybe that darkness was The River Man's true gift to her. Maybe that's why he thought of the foot as a trophy. Maybe he'd been the one to cut it off for her. Maybe Pete had. But she thought she remembered cutting it off herself. Maybe it had been a dream. Abby wasn't sure. She was never sure of anything. The only thing she knew with certainty was that Sissy mattered to her more than anyone else ever could. She loved Sissy more than she loved herself.

The River Man reached out for the foot, and when he took hold of it its deterioration accelerated. The decayed tissue blew away, revealing the bones beneath. They crumbled and disintegrated, and the ashes sunk into The River Man's pores. In one hand, the skin split and a jagged toenail sprouted from the wound—a new pick for his guitar strings, a tiny gravestone for the bluesman whose body was forever lost beneath that endless river of flesh.

That's when Lori snapped awake.

•••

They were leaving the firelight for a tunnel. No, not a tunnel—a doorway. A doorway that led to God knows where. To darkness. To nothingness.

Lori shivered in her cold, wet clothes, blinking away the water that ran down into her eyes. She recognized the arms around her as Abby's, and this confused her even further. It was Lori who helped Abby, not the other way around. This sudden role reversal made her teeth grind, but while she wanted to pull away from her sister, she felt too weak to do so. The River Man's words returned to her like remembering a vivid dream, and when she turned to take one last look inside his cabin, the door slammed shut before she could catch a glimpse of him. With the light of the wood-burning stove gone, there was only the unwelcoming blackness of the woods and the muted, crimson glow of that peppering of stars.

"It's okay, Sissy. We get to go home now."

But which home did she mean? The apartment that wasn't big enough for the both of them? Lori's *life* wasn't big enough for both of them anymore. Or did Abby mean the home they grew up in, the one Mom and Dad were forced to mortgage because of mounting hospital bills? That house had been the only place Lori had ever called home and meant it, for home was not just a building; it was a state of mind. Their parents' house, despite the evil things she'd done there, had been her last true home. Everything else was a diminishment. Though she tried to make nests for herself, they were never truly her own, partly because they were rentals, but more so because of Abby. She scattered her toys and clothing everywhere.

She left half-empty cereal bowls on the coffee table and dirty socks under the couch. A dog would have been less to clean up after than her sister was, and it made Lori's stomach tighten to live in such chaos. She kept the blinds closed so not to see it too well.

She wondered if her sister would have been such a slob had she not had her brain cracked, and the reminder of that dark day never failed to sting. It seemed that everything Abby ever did was a grim reminder of what Lori had done to her. She would never be free of it, and because she had never been caught, there could be no punishment, which meant no catharsis. And so her punishment came in a different form with the becoming of her big sister's guardian, a job that would continue until one of them died. No matter where they chose to live, it could never be a home. It was but a cage in a madhouse.

Her muscle control returning to her, Lori moved out of her sister's arms to walk on her own. Abby gathered their packs but did not put hers on. She took her flashlight out, but Lori knew it wasn't going to work. Not out here.

"It's dead," Abby said, her choice of words pinching Lori's neck. "Dead."

Now that Lori's eyes were adjusting, the glow of the stars was more potent, and she could make out the shadows of the trees and the gleaming rock at the edge of the cliff. She blinked when she noticed something moving there, a shimmer in the dark. Something was swaying from side to side, like the body of a man hung in a noose. She moved toward the cliff's edge.

Abby hadn't noticed. "Sissy? Does your flashlight work?"

Lori stared. The shape flickered between black and red, the light of the stars hitting it only when it wasn't swung below the branches of the towering, dead tree. The shadow was rectangular, and about the size of—

A plank swing.

Lori spotted the rope. The tree creaked softly as the swing

GONE TO SEE THE RIVER MAN

moved back and forth on the breeze. Even in the low light, she could see the mold and decay that had gathered on it. The sound of the river grew louder. Lori's breath caught in her throat as a white hand moved from behind the tree, fingers creeping like albino spider legs. Pete's withered face emerged, half hidden behind mossy bark.

"She wanted you to throw me in," he said. "But you didn't push me that day. You waited until I was ashes before you threw me in."

Lori couldn't find air to speak with. Her limbs shook. Her baby brother gave her one last smile, but it was a lonely one that faded as soon as it came. He tucked behind the tree again, first his face, then his fingers, crawling away into shadows.

"Sissy?"

Lori recognized her sister's voice, but something about it had changed. She turned around slowly, and with each turn of her head the golden light of day returned. Sunshine fell across everything she looked at, all the colors of nature returning. Light filled the woods, bringing the trees back to life. Their branches reached higher, lush green leaves rustling against a sky so blue it could only exist in summer. The River Man's shack was gone, replaced by a dirt path that led back home.

Abby was standing in the clearing where the trail ended, a beautiful teenage girl again. No crutches. No bent back or bowed legs. Backlit by the sun, her hair glowed in a solar flare, and her smile was even warmer than that sunshine. Abby was her own ghost. Undead more than alive. This image of her had been locked in Lori's mind all these years, clear as the old photographs she couldn't bear to look at. It was as if Lori had two sisters, one Abby born on the day of the other's death. Seeing the former Abby standing before her, Lori wondered which one she hated more: the young Abby who had been so much better than her in every way, or the crippled Abby who now chained her to an anti-life of misery and bad memories.

The River Man's words returned to her again.

Only you can tear down the walls. You must destroy the obstacle to free Edmund, and free yourself.

"Sissy?" Abby said, unbearably young and beautiful. "You ready?"

Lori nodded. She took her sister's hand and started toward the edge of the cliff. The forest on the other side pulsed with the all the dreams and promises of childhood, tearing something within her. There were no clouds, only that stunning blue sky. Gazing over the edge, the creek bubbled at the dip leading into the swimming hole and then flowed out the other side, winding into the distance, off to the river from which it sprung. There were fish and tadpoles below, birds and dragonflies above. Here there was life, and with life comes limitless possibilities. The promises of Lori's youth had been broken. The dreams had gone unfulfilled. But here there was renewed hope. The dream had always been of true love. With Edmund by her side, the dream would *become* the promise.

The sisters stood at the edge of the cliff, hand in hand. Lori turned to Abby, and for a moment she glimpsed the older, broken-down Abby within, all gray and cold, a dark aurora surrounding her, speckled by red freckles of light. Lori brushed her sister's face with the back of her hand, and the young Abby returned. Her cheek was warm, the skin perfect. Not a pimple or mole. Not even peach fuzz. Just soft, kissable flesh.

"You ready?" Abby asked again.

"I'm ready, Abby. Are you?"

Her sister nodded and looked out over the creek. It glistened like thousands of diamonds as Lori ran her hand across Abby's back, just as their mother had when trying to get the kids to sleep.

Finish what you started.

She put her other hand on Abby's back.

Lori pushed.

TWENTY-THREE

ABBY'S BLOOD SWIRLED IN THE pool, dripping from the rocks and broken shrubs. It poured from the holes in her body where snapping bones had pushed through the muscle, ripping free of the flesh. Her neck was a knot, her head all the way turned around so her dead eyes gazed up at her sister. Lori returned the empty stare.

The sunlight faded as clouds came out, ashen and wintry. A cold wind knifed through the trees and their leaves browned and fell to the earth. Beneath her feet, the grass crunched with frost. The world was dead again. She was back to the present, the reality from which she'd come.

She started down the mountain, leaving the backpacks and her sister's crutches behind.

Going downhill was much easier than going up, and without Abby slowing her down Lori made it to the bank within a couple of hours. In that time, she'd thought only of Edmund. After a lifetime of interference, the obstacle was now destroyed. She should have felt happiness or at least relief, but instead she felt hollowed out, cored. She was drained and dazed. But the happiness was sure to come. It had to. She just needed to be with Edmund again, and then the happiness would swell her heart. She had faith in them. Their love would clear her soul of all the things she'd tried so hard to forget.

Lori spotted the white birch tree they'd tied the boat to as she emerged from the woods. At the shoreline lay a body. She sighed, expecting Abby to have floated down on the current, but the corpse was too large to be her sister's. Its swollen belly reached for the clouds.

Buzz had been caught within a tangle of rocks and fallen branches. His carcass was on its back, legs dangling over a lip of stone. The stump of one leg dribbled blood into the water and his split head was swarming with insects. The river was its natural color, no longer red, except for the pocket he rested in. Lori stepped over the bloated carcass and toward the boat, giving the bow a shove until it bobbed on the water. Once she climbed in, she undid the rope and pulled the motor's cord. It resisted her. Her shoulder screamed with exhaustion and it took three more pulls for the boat to rumble back to life.

•••

It was near dark when she reached the spot they'd first departed from, back when there'd been three people in the boat. At least Lori thought it was the right spot. After hours on the river, the woods had become a repetitive, decaying blur. She turned the bow toward the shoreline, no longer caring about precautions to protect its structure. The boat hit the sand with a thud, wood cracking beneath her, and she stood up, climbed over the bow, and stepped upon the shore, grateful to be on land again. She didn't want to see another river for as long as she lived, but if there was a hell, she was sure this goddamn river would be waiting there for her.

Lori started up the trail. There was still a long trek to the car. She may not reach it until dawn, especially in her exhausted state. Maybe she could sleep in Buzz's shack for the night and start fresh in the morning. Would that big dog let her in without Buzz or would it try to bite her face off? It was bound to be hungry and would stay that way if it remained locked in there. But it was big enough to break down the door and learn to hunt rabbits when starvation became a real threat.

Lori sighed. She was cold, tired and hungry, and yet she felt the need to press on. She was out of the river. Now she needed out of Killen. The sooner she got back to her apartment, the sooner she could visit Varden Prison. She was so close to putting decades of misery behind her. On the other side of this cursed mountain, there was joy, pure and deep and uncompromised. She had earned it, hadn't she? After all she'd been through, did she not deserve the greatest treasure life offered? Love was just beyond the tree line. A true sense of home was once again a possibility. She'd proven her devotion. She was *number one*. No longer could Niko stand in her way, and Lori trumped any other slutty bitches that may want to interfere. Edmund was completely hers now, body and soul. And he was waiting for her.

I will love, honor and obey you, always.

It began to rain.

She pressed on.

•••

There were whispers in the dark. She could hear them even with the rain coming down. Voices she knew but hadn't heard in years. But she couldn't make out their words as they muttered in the shadows. Her mother was weeping. Dad was talking too fast, the way he always had when he was worried.

"Shut up," Lori hissed back. "You can't stand in the way of my happiness anymore. Things are different now."

But the only thing that muted their voices was the occasional rumble of thunder. It rolled through Killen like spreading fire, and Lori was grateful for these brief interruptions. The rain was freezing and her toes and fingers had gone numb, but the storm at least provided her with moments of lucidity. These ghosts would not be able to follow her out of this place. Death belonged here.

She slipped in the mud every now and then, but kept on walking, following the trail they'd come in on. Even once the rain faded, the storm clouds covered the moon, leaving her in unrelenting darkness. Still she pressed on, going by feel. Her back and hips ached. She was famished, exhausted and cold. One of her boots had a tear that was letting water in. Her body begged for sleep. But still she pushed herself, hiking until the first sliver of dawn split the horizon.

By the time she saw him, dawn had come in full, a dull, gray beginning to her last day in Killen. The rain dissipated. The man seemed to grow taller as he moved up the trail, his ape arms swinging at his sides. His black suit was wrinkled but dry, unlike Lori's sopping clothes, and it hung upon him like a blanket, two sizes too large.

When he looked up at her, he tilted his hat in a hello.

Lori kept walking. There was no one to hide from the Deacon now. He stopped when they were close, and she stopped too, not knowing why. She felt as if she had something to say or prove but didn't know what.

The old man flashed a yellow smile. "Looks like your journey's done come to an end, child."

She nodded but had no words.

The man's eyes were jaundiced. They dilated as he spoke. "Only now ya travel alone. But, like I say, no one *really* travels this here river alone, now do they?"

The words fell from her mouth like sand. "No. No, they don't."

"Must've had a real nice visit."

She nodded.

"Got whatcha wanted, I reckon. I see it in your eyes. I saw that look in my own eyes once, when I was baptizin' my children. The river was reflectin' my image back at me. And in my face I saw what I see on yours right now, child." His skeletal grimace twisted into a wider smile. "Ya done good. Ya done it *right*."

The Deacon leaned in, as if sniffing her. When his hands went to

GONE TO SEE THE RIVER MAN

Lori's shoulders, she did not flinch or pull away. Her stare never wavered.

"I'm glad ya had such a nice visit, child."

They were silent.

Lori spoke. "I'm done here. Don't think I'll be seein' you again."

"No, probably not at that. But I'll be seein' you, I'm sure. In the papers, like the others."

Lori didn't reply. She looked into the distance, spotting a glint of chrome. Thank God, the car was still where she'd parked it. She was almost out of here.

"Now go on," The Deacon said. "Time to get whatcha done earned. What ya deserve."

With a click of a laugh, the old man shuffled on and the woods lining the trail seemed to bend toward him, cocooning him in Killen forever. He tilted his head to their branches and sang in horse rhapsody.

"Yes, we'll gather at the river! The beautiful, beautiful river! Gather with the man at the river. Runs red with all our blood."

Lori passed by the sign that had welcomed her upon arrival. The past was the past. It couldn't hurt her anymore. She opened the car and climbed inside, flicking on the heat before she'd even started the engine. The radio came on, loud and broken by static. Hadn't she turned it off before they'd arrived? Ragged blues music made the speakers crackle, a slide guitar strumming, a death moan floating over it like smoke. She turned the dial so hard the plastic nob snapped off. The music faded to a murmur but remained until she'd driven out of Killen. Then there was only silence. In the rearview mirror, the woods grew blacker, smaller, until they no longer existed.

A voice startled Lori. A newswoman had come on the radio, soft beneath the static.

"State police have sealed off the area..."

Sealed off what area? Lori didn't need traffic stops keeping her from getting home. She reached for what remained of the busted dial and managed to raise the volume.

"Sources have confirmed that most of the escapees have been captured, but the manhunt continues for one prisoner who managed to break free during the riot that began here at Varden Prison yesterday afternoon."

Lori gasped. Her knuckles went white on the wheel.

"The man's name has not been released as of yet—"

But Lori already knew. She could feel it in her heart and loins—a warm, new hope.

"—he is described as a highly dangerous individual, and should be considered armed, as many of the overpowered prison guards lost their weapons during the riot. Again, this is being called one of the most brutal prison riots in decades, with the death toll now at seventeen, and dozens injured."

Tears of joy clouded Lori's vision. She laughed excitedly. The River Man had wasted no time. Her long, grueling journey had been worth all its terror and suffering. Her sacrifices had not been made in vain. She'd proven herself to Edmund Cox, and now he was rushing to her open arms. She knew it with every fiber, every sense. He was too clever to be caught now that he was free. It was likely he who had started the riot, the distraction making it easier for him to act upon an escape plan he'd been crafting for some time. Just as she had journeyed through violence and darkness for him, he was now on such a voyage for her. The power of their love was the only compass they needed, a lighthouse beacon in the darkness their lives had been without one another. That darkness was almost over now. This was really happening.

Lori beamed at her reflection in the mirror.

"So this is what happiness feels like."

TWENTY-FOUR

LORI MANAGED TO AVOID THE roadblocks and traffic stops the police had set up. She thought about doing a manhunt of her own, but decided it was best to go straight home. Edmund had her address. It was on every one of the letters she'd written him. He would come to her safely. The police couldn't stop them, couldn't find them. She'd made their love invincible. No more obstacles. Abby was dead. The walls of the prison had been broken. Now they could run away to Montreal, to Cabo San Lucas, to anywhere.

She took the stairs up to her floor and her footsteps echoed down the empty hall. It was cold here, but she would be warm soon enough. Edmund would see to that. He'd take her in his arms and lay her down and enter her. She felt a sudden heat just thinking about it. Hopefully there would be time to clean herself up. She wanted to be bathed and shaved for her king. A little makeup and perfume. Lingerie. Start things off right.

When she came to her door, she realized there would be no time for that, but she was too excited to feel any disappointment. The door stood ajar. Small, red dots speckled the doormat and doorknob, still wet. Lori hoped the blood wasn't his. She didn't want her sweet Edmund to ever hurt. Love flushed her cheeks as she opened wide the door and stepped into the kitchen. It was empty, but there were more red droplets on the floor and counter. She quickly closed the door behind her.

"Edmund?" she called out. But she couldn't seem to speak higher than a whisper.

She came into the living room. Something had happened here. The coffee table was overturned, glistening with more blood, much more. Half the couch cushions were on the floor and one curtain hung by a single loop from the rod, the rest ripped off. An empty bottle of vodka had been smashed on the floor.

"Edmund?" she called out, louder this time.

Her flesh tingled as she followed the bloody footprints in the rug. Some were large, like a man's feet. The others were smaller and bloodier. The closer they came to the hallway, the more smeared they became, as if whoever the smaller footprints belonged to had been dragged. In the hall, the blood was thick enough to cover the carpet entirely, a wet path of gore. It ran through her apartment like a river, a crimson river of flesh, and she followed it, knowing it for what it was, knowing she belonged on it, that she would never truly leave it.

The door to her bedroom was slightly ajar. Pale light bled through the crack, along with an odor Lori had gotten used to but still hated. It smelled of the cellar where she'd found the dead woman. It smelled like The River Man's shack, wallpapered in human flesh. When a shadow moved behind the door, Lori felt suddenly cold again, but couldn't explain why. She knew who was in there, but somehow that wasn't bringing her the joy she'd felt since hearing the news of the prison break. Why hadn't he come out when she'd called him? Why hadn't he leapt at the chance to hold her in his arms?

"Edmund?"

A voice like sandpaper on skin. "Come on in."

Her chest grew warm again.

"I've been waitin' on you," he said.

GONE TO SEE THE RIVER MAN

She wet her lips for the kiss she'd been dying for and swung the door in, a teen girl greeting her prom date. But when she saw Edmund sitting on the edge of the bed, her mouth instantly went dry. Lori stopped in the doorway—frozen, blank, dead inside. For all the horror she should have felt, instead she felt nothing. It was all too much. She'd hadn't been able to take it all in yet.

Edmund sat at the edge of the bed, naked but for a thick coat of blood matted in his chest hair and covering his arms like long gloves. In his lap was Niko's severed head. Her tongue was hanging out, purple and swollen. Many of her teeth were broken. Edmund cradled the skull with one hand and stroked her long, black hair with the other, as if the head were a kitten. He smiled at Lori.

"Don't be jealous, now. I done been in the joint too long. A man has needs."

Lori realized she hadn't been breathing. "You . . . you brought her here?"

"Nah, darlin'. I called her and told her to come on over. See, I came here soon as I broke out. Was hopin' you'd be here but the place was empty."

"I was . . . at the river."

"I figured. Seein' The River Man takes time. But ya musta done right by him, cause here we are."

Lori struggled to look into his eyes—lost, uncertain. "Why did you have Niko come here?"

"Now I done told ya not to get jealous. I needed somethin' to hold me over. A woman. Flesh."

Edmund stood, letting the head roll to the floor. Lori followed it with her eyes, for the first time noticing the nude, headless corpse crushed up into the corner, a wad of human remains. Its arms and legs were bent and broken, reminding her of Abby, of things she wasn't supposed to be reminded of anymore.

Edmund stepped closer. "Been too long since I fucked and killed."

Lori tried to keep her whimpers silent. She failed. She began to tremble. But despite the truth that was growing more and more apparent, she did not try to run. She loved Edmund. That was all she had to hold on to, no matter the cost.

"You know you're my favorite," he said. "Niko was only willing until we got down to it. Then she got scared and started screamin'. Hell, she shoulda known what this was. Shoulda known what I am. Just another disappointment like all the others. But not you, Lori. You've come so far. I know you won't let me down. You're *willing*. Truly willing to do whatever it takes. That's how I know you're the one."

Edmund wiped away her tears and she gazed into his eyes, seeing a tenderness that had never been there before. She realized then that he truly loved her. There was no hate in what he was about to do. What most would see as cruelties were actually signs of the deepest affection he could muster. Violence was his love letter. Death was all his soul.

There's only two places anyone can find peace—the woods and the grave.

She'd truly won his heart, the first thing she'd ever won in her life, the only thing that mattered now that she was at the end of it.

Lori began undressing and Edmund reached for the butcher knife on top of the dresser. He'd chosen a clean one just for her. Once she was fully naked, he stepped in close, their bare flesh touching at long last for one beautiful, fatal moment.

"Will it hurt, darling?" she asked.

Edmund flicked the blade with his finger. "Love always does."

Thanks to Norman Prentiss, CV Hunt, Andresen Prunty, John Wayne Comunale, Bryan Smith, Tangie Silva, Ryan Harding, Josh Doherty, Brian Keene, Wrath James White, Edward Lee, Christine Morgan, Bernard DeBenedictis, Chad Stroup, Gregg Kirby, Nicole Amburgey, Mary Sangiovanni, John Boden, Wesley Southard, Katie Southard, John McNee, Paul Goblirsch, Tod Clark, and Jack Ketchum (RIP).

The River Man is pleased with you all.

Biggest of thanks to Bear.

Enormous thanks to Junior Kimbrough, R.L. Burnside, Lead Belly, Robert Johnson, Howlin' Wolf, and Buddy Guy, whose music inspired this novel and became its soundtrack as I wrote it.

Deep thanks to Nick Drake for his somber song "River Man", which was the launching impetus for this cosmic horror.

And special thanks to Tom Mumme—always.

Kristopher Triana is the Splatterpunk Award-winning author of *Full Brutal*. His other horror titles include *Gone to See the River Man*, *Blood Relations*, *They All Died Screaming* and many other terrifying books. He's also the author of the crime thrillers *The Ruin Season* and *Shepherd of the Black Sheep*. His work has been published in multiple languages and has drawn praise from the likes of *Publisher's Weekly*, *Rue Morgue Magazine*, *Cemetery Dance*, *Scream Magazine*, *The Horror Fiction Review* and many more.

He lives in a cold, dark place somewhere in New England.

Other Grindhouse Press Titles

#666__*Satanic Summer* by Andersen Prunty
#070__*Horrorama* edited by C.V. Hunt
#069__*Depraved 4* by Bryan Smith
#068__*Worst Laid Plans: An Anthology of Vacation Horror* edited by Samantha Kolesnik
#067__*Deathtripping: Collected Horror Stories* by Andersen Prunty
#066__*Depraved* by Bryan Smith
#065__*Crazytimes* by Scott Cole
#064__*Blood Relations* by Kristopher Triana
#063__*The Perfectly Fine House* by Stephen Kozeniewski and Wile E. Young
#062__*Savage Mountain* by John Quick
#061__*Cocksucker* by Lucas Milliron
#060__*Luciferin* by J. Peter W.
#059__*The Fucking Zombie Apocalypse* by Bryan Smith
#058__*True Crime* by Samantha Kolesnik
#057__*The Cycle* by John Wayne Comunale
#056__*A Voice So Soft* by Patrick Lacey
#055__*Merciless* by Bryan Smith
#054__*The Long Shadows of October* by Kristopher Triana
#053__*House of Blood* by Bryan Smith
#052__*The Freakshow* by Bryan Smith
#051__*Dirty Rotten Hippies and Other Stories* by Bryan Smith
#050__*Rites of Extinction* by Matt Serafini
#049__*Saint Sadist* by Lucas Mangum
#048__*Neon Dies at Dawn* by Andersen Prunty
#047__*Halloween Fiend* by C.V. Hunt
#046__*Limbs: A Love Story* by Tim Meyer
#045__*As Seen On T.V.* by John Wayne Comunale
#044__*Where Stars Won't Shine* by Patrick Lacey
#043__*Kinfolk* by Matt Kurtz

#042__*Kill For Satan!* by Bryan Smith
#041__*Dead Stripper Storage* by Bryan Smith
#040__*Triple Axe* by Scott Cole
#039__*Scummer* by John Wayne Comunale
#038__*Cockblock* by C.V. Hunt
#037__*Irrationalia* by Andersen Prunty
#036__*Full Brutal* by Kristopher Triana
#035__*Office Mutant* by Pete Risley
#034__*Death Pacts and Left-Hand Paths* by John Wayne Comunale
#033__*Home Is Where the Horror Is* by C.V. Hunt
#032__*This Town Needs A Monster* by Andersen Prunty
#031__*The Fetishists* by A.S. Coomer
#030__*Ritualistic Human Sacrifice* by C.V. Hunt
#029__*The Atrocity Vendor* by Nick Cato
#028__*Burn Down the House and Everyone In It* by Zachary T. Owen
#027__*Misery and Death and Everything Depressing* by C.V. Hunt
#026__*Naked Friends* by Justin Grimbol
#025__*Ghost Chant* by Gina Ranalli
#024__*Hearers of the Constant Hum* by William Pauley III
#023__*Hell's Waiting Room* by C.V. Hunt
#022__*Creep House: Horror Stories* by Andersen Prunty
#021__*Other People's Shit* by C.V. Hunt
#020__*The Party Lords* by Justin Grimbol
#019__*Sociopaths In Love* by Andersen Prunty
#018__*The Last Porno Theater* by Nick Cato
#017__*Zombieville* by C.V. Hunt
#016__*Samurai Vs. Robo-Dick* by Steve Lowe
#015__*The Warm Glow of Happy Homes* by Andersen Prunty
#014__*How To Kill Yourself* by C.V. Hunt
#013__*Bury the Children in the Yard: Horror Stories* by Andersen Prunty

#012__*Return to Devil Town (Vampires in Devil Town Book Three)* by Wayne Hixon
#011__*Pray You Die Alone: Horror Stories* by Andersen Prunty
#010__*King of the Perverts* by Steve Lowe
#009__*Sunruined: Horror Stories* by Andersen Prunty
#008__*Bright Black Moon (Vampires in Devil Town Book Two)* by Wayne Hixon
#007__*Hi I'm a Social Disease: Horror Stories* by Andersen Prunty
#006__*A Life On Fire* by Chris Bowsman
#005__*The Sorrow King* by Andersen Prunty
#004__*The Brothers Crunk* by William Pauley III
#003__*The Horribles* by Nathaniel Lambert
#002__*Vampires in Devil Town* by Wayne Hixon
#001__*House of Fallen Trees* by Gina Ranalli
#000__*Morning is Dead* by Andersen Prunty